D1083836

THE SECRET OF CASTLEGATE MANOR

THE SECRET OF CASTLEGATE MANOR

•

Karen Cogan

AVALON BOOKS
NEW YORK

To the memory of Sally Cogan,
who always enjoyed a good romance.

Chapter One

Caroline stared past the velvet curtain of the hackney window, trying to calm the panic that grew with each passing mile. How had she let Lady Eleanor talk her into this mad deception? Her memory played back the last details of their conversation as Lady Eleanor lay ill and pale, having barely the strength to hold onto Caroline's hand.

Lady Eleanor's lips barely moved as she whispered, "You are nearly nineteen, are you not?"

Caroline nodded.

"This may be your only chance, my dear."

Caroline sighed. Perhaps her elderly employer had been right. The covetous relatives had arrived just before the dear lady died. They would not have abided having any of the estate bequeathed upon a young abigail in gratitude for the years she had cared for her mistress.

A cough racked the lady's frail body. Caroline waited,

kneeling patiently beside the bed until her mistress was able to continue.

"If only I could leave you something . . . But of course Adela would attain a solicitor to prove you had taken advantage of my frail faculties." Her eyebrows puckered in disapproval at the thought of her daughter-in-law, and her frown deepened. "Perhaps they would even have you arrested."

Caroline shuddered. The thought was appalling. She patted Lady Eleanor's hand. "You have been generous to me, my lady. Another mistress might have turned me out after my parents were killed."

Lady Eleanor's eyes lit with determination as she whispered her conspiracy to Caroline. "You know, dear, after your parents died, you became much more than a maid to me. You have become a dear companion. I want more for you than becoming a servant to Adela. I have written a letter of introduction to my niece, Lady Aberly, who lives at the country estate. Upon my death you are to go there and present yourself as my great-niece. You will take along the carriage money that I have set aside for you. You must choose some dresses from my wardrobe that would be suitable attire. Then, secret yourself in your chamber to alter them."

Lady Eleanor coughed. "A young lady traveling alone will raise questions. So you must say that I had planned to come with you. Then you may explain that my death made it impossible for Adela to spare an abigail to travel with you."

Caroline bit her lip. "My lady, such deceit. If I should ever be found out . . ."

"It is not deceit. You are a more fitting relative than those who are truly my kin. You must go to the country and find a young squire. Marry well, Caroline. I want this for you."

Lady Eleanor had closed her eyes. The tired lines on her face told Caroline that arguing would exact a tremendous toll on the frail old woman. As Caroline rose to slip from the room, Lady Eleanor whispered, "Promise me, Caroline. Promise me you will do this."

Caroline hesitated at the door. What real choice did she have? Perhaps Adela would keep her on, though it would be tedious employment with the over-strung, shrewish woman. If she did not keep her on, Caroline would be forced to seek another serving position.

Lady Eleanor lived only another week. Caroline used the time when she was not sitting with her or attending to Adela's numerous demands to alter the wardrobe suitable for a woman of rank. She stayed on another week after the funeral. But a week of Lady Adela was enough to convince Caroline she would have nothing but misery in the only home she had ever known.

She gave her notice and packed up to leave London. She shared the hired coach with two elderly matrons who, fortunately, preferred sleeping to talking.

They stopped overnight at a comfortable little inn in Reading where Caroline parted with a few shilling for room and board. Though she had always been frugal, she knew her earnings would not go far should she be found out and cast on her own.

Now, as the coach rocked down the well-traveled road

outside Bath, Caroline stared across the verdant grasses and riotous flowers, trying to catch a first glimpse of the estate.

As they rounded a bend, she gasped at the sight of Castlegate Manor. Though Lady Eleanor had described the Georgian structure in detail, she was not prepared for the size of the gray stone house that loomed before her. It seemed to stretch a London city block. Its windows looked out upon her like a hundred curious eyes.

The coach drew to a halt before the massive polished door. The coachman helped her down the steps while the footman collected the impedimenta of her journey.

Caroline clutched her reticule tightly as a servant in proper white, starched shirt opened the door. He inclined his head slightly in courtesy and waited for her to speak.

"I am Miss Caroline Stewart, great-niece of Lady Eleanor Stewart. I believe a letter was sent regarding my arrival."

Caroline had rehearsed this to herself a hundred times during her journey, fearing she would not remember her new surname was now Stewart and not Greene. She licked her dry lips and wished she had stayed in London.

The butler moved aside. "If you will come this way, miss, I will alert Lady Aberly of your arrival."

Caroline followed the butler from the wide entryway into the great room. Heavy damask draperies of verdant green at the windows had been pulled to let in the afternoon sun. The doors opened to a rose garden with trimmed hedges that wound into such a maze that Caroline was sure she would become lost should she ever venture into them.

She surveyed the portraits which hung on the walls. One young woman bore such a striking similarity to Lady Eleanor that she was sure it must have been painted in her youth. Other portraits bore family resemblances, most of them men in military uniforms or stiff riding clothes and dark-haired women with brown eyes.

Perhaps, at least with her chestnut curls and dark eyes, Caroline would not be immediately spotted as an impostor. She bit her lip, wishing she had not agreed to this scheme.

She had waited only a moment when a rustle of skirts alerted her of the arrival of her hostess. Caroline turned to meet her, forcing a smile, though she feared the pounding of her heart would drown out any words of greeting.

Lady Aberly paused, her smile lingering on her lips as she glanced about the room. "You must be Miss Stewart. But where, dear, is your great-aunt?" Lady Aberly's gaze flitted about the room as though Caroline might be hiding the elderly lady.

Caroline rested a gloved hand upon the Queen Anne chair to steady herself, hoping her knees would not buckle as she tested her new role. "My great-aunt has just died this last week. Her last wish was that I proceed without her."

The stout lady hastened to offer Caroline a chair. "No wonder you have gone so pale. I had not heard of our loss. Lady Eleanor was my aunt, you know."

Caroline nodded. "I grew very fond of her in the time I knew her."

Lady Aberly fixed Caroline with her small dark eyes.

Did Caroline detect suspicion in her gaze? "Your aunt's letter stated you had recently arrived from India. I knew her youngest brother resided there, but I quite lost track of the names of his grandchildren. How is your grandfather, dear? It must have been hard to leave your family. Still, I cannot think how you ever stood that wretched climate."

Caroline swallowed hard. She knew very little about India, including the climate. "Grandfather is fine and India is very warm." She smoothed the folds of her muslin skirt and avoided Lady Aberly's eyes.

"But I am forgetting my manners. You must be famished, my dear. I shall ring for tea."

Caroline settled gratefully into silence while the tea was brought in by the same straight-backed butler who had answered the door.

Lady Aberly dismissed the butler and, with acquired skill, poured the tea.

A rustling in the doorway announced a feminine arrival.

Caroline glanced up to see a young woman of about her age hesitate at the sight of a guest.

Lady Aberly smiled at the girl. Speaking to Caroline she said, "Miss Stewart, I would like to acquaint you with my daughter, Miss Lavenia. Lavenia, Miss Caroline has arrived from London. She is the great-niece of my newly departed Aunt Eleanor. She is here to stay with us."

Lavenia curtsied gracefully. Caroline titled her head in shy acknowledgement. Though she had delivered tea to ladies, and been privy to overhearing polite conversation, she had never had occasion to practice such a skill.

Lavenia's day dress of soft rose mull swished as she slid into her chair. "I suppose that makes us cousins. I have never had a female cousin reside with us."

Lady Aberly clucked in disapproval. "That sounded somehow improper, my dear."

Lavenia's face, comely despite her angular jaw, pulled to a pout. "I only meant that my cousin, Steffen Humphrey, was little enough company while he was here."

Lady Aberly's face flushed. "We shall not speak of that, but rather of our guest. Did you have a difficult journey? I am afraid I would have succumbed to lingering vapors had I to deal with the fear of highwaymen."

Caroline's eyes met those of her hostess as she answered honestly, "The road was well-traveled, my lady. I think there was little enough danger."

Lavenia wiped her lips delicately after taking a bite of her small cake. "I have not been to London in ages, but I do remember it was unbearably hot in the summer." Her voice held a hint of complaint.

Caroline nodded. "That has not changed, I assure you."

Lavenia leaned forward, an eager light in her dark eyes. "You must tell us about the fashions. I know only what I have seen on the streets of Bath."

Caroline knew enough about fashion from attending Lady Eleanor on her numerous shopping expeditions to satisfy the curiosity of her two hostesses.

Lavenia cast her mother a longing look. "I shall have

to have a trip into Bath soon. My favorite bonnet is becoming frayed and I shall not be able to wear it again."

Lady Aberly looked thoughtful. "Perhaps it is good Miss Stewart has arrived. You could, perhaps, be proper companions to one another, since it is not seemly for a young woman to be out alone."

Lady Aberly fixed Caroline with what she feared to be a look of reproof for her lack of an attendant upon arrival. Caroline decided to pretend ignorance of the remark. "I would be happy to peruse the local shops. I have need of very little at the moment, but I should be happy to help your daughter in her search for a new bonnet."

Caroline hoped she would not be required to spend her savings in order to keep up appearances.

"Oh, that would be lovely," said Lavenia, her eyes alight. "Would Wednesday be too early to travel again? I know you have had a long journey."

Caroline shook her head. "A day of rest will be enough. I look forward to the outing."

Lady Aberly studied the two young women. Caroline could not help thinking a comparison was taking place. She wished she had an inkling as to the thoughts forming behind the thick-lashed dark eyes.

The lady smiled. "Then it is all settled. I shall tell Edwards to advise John Coachman to be available. Now, I know you must be very tired. I shall ring for a maid to show you to your room."

An upstairs maid appeared. Lady Aberly spoke firmly. "Maggie, see to Miss Stewart's comfort. She will be staying with us for awhile."

Maggie curtsied smartly. "Yes, m'lady."

She smiled shyly at Caroline. "This way, if you please, Miss."

Caroline followed Maggie up the wide formal staircase that wound to the second floor. They passed down a long hall, then turned a corner. Maggie opened the first door.

Caroline caught her breath. The formal sitting room held a small settee, two Queen Anne chairs with exquisitely embroidered seats, and a small writing desk.

The massive bed and matching wardrobe sat on a fine rug of red and gold. A starched muslin skirt of pale blue adorned the dressing table. Never had Caroline imagined herself to be quartered in such a room. Compared to the attic servant quarters in Lady Eleanor's London house, which had been adequate if somewhat drafty, this room was palatial.

She felt panic surfacing, sure she could never keep up the charade. She was trained to attend, not be attended. She would surely slip up.

Maggie waited beside the door. "Will you be requiring anything at the moment, Miss?"

Caroline shook her head. Relief washed over her as Maggie left the room, closing the door softly behind her.

Caroline placed her bonnet and gloves on the table beside the bed and opened the armoire. Her clothes had been unpacked and carefully hung. How many times had she done this task for guests who visited Lady Eleanor?

She strode to the window, which had been opened to air the room with the gentle summer breeze. The land rolled in a graceful carpet of green. Harebells mingled their blue tops in the verdant lawn. The scent of meadowsweet hung in the air.

She had been very young in the days when Lady Eleanor made trips to this estate, and had not been invited along. And in the last few years, the dear lady had been too frail to travel.

Caroline's childhood had been confined to the streets of London. She would have loved, as a child, to walk the distant woods that joined these green fields, to have run among the flowers. Though her servant status would have prohibited such frivolity, she might have accompanied the lady on walks.

She shook off her silly attachment to the countryside. Previous visits would have made her current pretense impossible. She would have been known to Lady Aberly. Her only chance of living as one of the country gentry would be to keep up this masquerade.

And yet, the deception bothered her conscience. She had been raised by parents who placed high regard for the truth. Only her desire for a better life and Lady Eleanor's dying wish could have caused her to chance this impersonation. Still, something in the back of her mind warned her that her deception would come with a price.

She stretched across the high bed and felt her aching muscles, jostled by long miles in the coach, begin to relax. She closed her eyes, intending only to rest, and awoke with a start at a soft knock at the door.

Maggie peeked in. "Will you be requiring help in dressing for the evening meal, Miss?"

Caroline shook her head. "No thank you, Maggie. I shall be able to manage."

She washed at the lovely china basin with painted pink roses and dried herself on the spotless white towel. Feeling refreshed, she slipped out of her rumpled traveling dress and into a soft aqua gown of jaconet. Working quickly, she piled her dark hair onto her head and pinned it neatly in place. After pinching her cheeks and dusting her freshly washed face with rice powder, she stepped resolutely into the hall.

She paused, hand on the banister, feeling paralyzed by the sudden worry of who else might join them for dinner. Was there a Lord of Castlegate Manor? Would he see though her pretense and send her packing?

With these questions causing her heart to flutter, she forced herself to descend the winding staircase. Edwards, the butler, met her at the bottom. He escorted her to the dining room where Lady Aberly and Lavenia sat at the far end of the massive table.

She was seated to Lady Aberly's right, across from Lavenia. Since Lady Aberly presided at the end of the table, Caroline could only assume there either was no lord of the manor or that he was away at the moment.

"I trust you are somewhat refreshed from your trip?" Lady Aberly asked.

Caroline nodded. "Quite rested." She hoped the ladies did not notice the way her hands shook as she attempted to remember all her table manners.

The meal was sumptuous: several meats, a choice of breads, and fruit for desert. Still, Caroline found it difficult to taste what was put before her as she responded to the polite conversation.

"I hear there is to be an intimate gathering at Madam Ruyter's house after the concert next week," Lavenia reported.

"And we have been invited to attend," added Lady Aberly.

She turned to Caroline. "We procured the tickets to the concert before you arrived, but we would like nothing better than to have you join us. I understand the soprano is of some renown in London. I wonder if you have heard of her."

Caroline shook her head quickly. "I doubt that, my lady. I was in London such a short time before Lady . . . my great-aunt died. I spent most of my time attending to her." That part, at least, was not a lie.

"A pity you arrived to find Lady Eleanor ill. I know her. She would have enjoyed introducing you to London society," Lady Aberly stated.

Caroline, despite her discomfiture, had to choke down the urge to laugh. The vision of Lady Eleanor introducing her servant to the socials of London made too comical a picture to entertain.

"Perhaps the eligible young men who will attend Madam Ruyter's gathering will be of interest to you." Lavenia's eyes danced as she goaded Caroline. Yet, Caroline detected no malice in her tone.

"I shall be glad to meet whomever your friend has invited," Caroline answered politely, though her feelings differed greatly from her words. Such a gathering and the ensuing prospect of meeting a suitable man was exactly what she had come here to achieve. However, the actual prospect filled her with trepidation.

Lady Aberly nodded politely. "We shall see that a ticket is acquired for you."

Was there distrust in Lady Aberly's expression? Caroline decided she must be imagining it. She had not made a fatal error that she knew of as yet.

Still, she could not let down her guard. One mistake could expose her. She must proceed with extreme caution.

Chapter Two

Caroline woke the next morning, glad for a day of rest. For the first time in her life, she took breakfast in her room, then allowed Maggie to help her into a fresh muslin dress.

She considered the question that had been on her mind. Deciding to put it to Maggie, she asked offhandedly, "Is the master of the estate away at the present? I haven not met him yet."

Maggie paused in her ministrations. "The master, Miss?" She seemed to be considering.

"Yes. There is a Lord Aberly, is there not?" She could not politely inquire this of Lady Aberly, but she could ask her servant.

"No, Miss. I understand Lord Aberly died before the Lady and Miss Lavenia came to live here. I never met him, Miss."

Caroline nodded. So Lady Aberly was a widow. She

wondered if the lady was of independent means or a poor relative of Lady Eleanor.

Edwards greeted her politely as she passed through the great room on her way to the rose garden. The sunshine glinted on dewy petals as she closed her eyes and bent to inhale the heavenly scent. She would be happy to spend her life ensconced in this garden.

She followed the cobbled path of high hedges rising behind a variety of roses until she reached a stone bench. She sat down, letting her bonnet shade her face. Alone in this quiet place, she closed her eyes and invented a fictional past that pleased her. She envisioned herself as a child being taken for walks in the woods, as a young girl with a governess, learning French and deportment.

No doubt Lavenia had known these privileges, while maids such as Caroline had fetched water for baths and mended pretty clothes.

Caroline closed her eyes and breathed in the sweet scent of the garden. Her fantasy of a childhood fled with the reminder that had Lady Aberly known the truth, she would never have been allowed to sit at table discussing theater and intimate parties. She harbored no bitterness for her past. Her parents had been kind and good. Yet, now that she had come here, she knew this was where she longed to stay. Like Cinderella, it was the dream of her childhood.

A shadow blocked the sun. Caroline opened her eyes, startled to see a young man paused in the path, staring down at her. His face held a mixture of curiosity and suspicion.

He swept off his hat and bowed in response to her startled gaze. "I held my breath lest I interrupt such rapt reflection on so fair a face. I am Steffen Humphrey, Viscount of Crestwood. Whom do I have the pleasure of meeting?"

Caroline searched her memory for when she had heard the name. Then she remembered. Lavenia had said he was the cousin who had visited the estate.

She smiled. "I am Miss Caroline Stewart, great-niece of Lady Eleanor."

She watched the expression in his dark eyes flicker. Was there something calculating in their depths?

He rubbed his finely chiseled chin. "I was not aware that Lady Eleanor had another great-niece."

Caroline felt her composure flicker. She swallowed down her discomfort. "I have been abroad, sir."

A gracious smile formed on his thin lips. "I see. I just heard of the dear lady's passing. My man and I have come to see to the condition of the estate. He nodded to the servant who waited behind him. "Without the firm hand of a master, I feared to find it in disrepair."

Caroline shook her head. "No, indeed, my lord. The house is in grand form and the gardens are a delight." She took in his impeccable clothes, his fine silken waistcoat, his finely woven coat.

He nodded. "I am glad to hear it. My business interests have occupied me and it has been quite some time since my last visit."

He extended his hand. "Pray lend me your company. Edwards has informed Lady Aberly of my presence and I was just going in for tea."

Caroline extended her gloved hand and allowed him to assist her in rising. They strolled the cobblestone path back to the great room.

The tea and biscuits had been laid out upon the polished table. Lady Aberly and Lavenia were already seated.

Lady Aberly smiled, her dark eyes taking in the arrival of the Viscount with Caroline. "An unexpected pleasure, my lord. I see you have met our cousin."

"Indeed, and found her most charming."

Caroline felt her cheeks flush with the unaccustomed attention. "I was admiring the roses when Mr. Humphrey happened into the garden."

Lady Aberly poured tea. "How did you find the garden, sir?"

Lord Steffen Humphrey accepted his cup. "Most ably kept."

Caroline thought she detected a note of disappointment in his voice.

He continued. "My housing in the Royal Crescent is not without comfort. Yet, I have always harbored a fondness for this estate."

Caroline noticed how Lavenia's hand shook as she sipped her tea. His words seemed to cause her discomfit. Caroline, however, could understand his sentiments. Though she had been here a short time, she also held a fondness for this fine old house, its forest, and green expanse of lawn.

Lady Aberly chatted into the momentary silence. "You are most welcome here any time. Lavenia made mention of you only yesterday."

Lavenia's eyes went wide before she regained her composure.

Lord Humphrey eyed her appraisingly. "I am honored, for you must know with what high regard I hold my cousin."

He let his gaze drift to Caroline. "And now I find I have another comely cousin. A choice, now I see."

Caroline felt keenly the competition in which she was being thrown with Lavenia. In all her days of serving, she had never felt the sting of being a thoroughbred led through the ring for bidding. She disliked the feeling. And she was beginning to dislike the viscount.

She tossed her head. "I assure you, sir, my position as a temporary guest will not disturb any choices you may have made."

Lord Humphrey dabbed his mouth with the edge of the pale linen napkin. "We shall see. Now, as I have business back in Bath, I shall thank you ladies for your fine company."

He bowed over Lady Aberly's hand and nodded his good-byes. "So nice to meet you, Miss Stewart. I am sure we shall meet again soon."

Caroline extended her good wishes, feeling a tangible relief sweep over the room at his departure.

She puzzled over the possible understanding between Lavenia and the Viscount as she took her afternoon rest, finally falling asleep longer than she intended. On the way to late tea, she paused at the drawing room. Without endeavoring to eavesdrop, she could clearly hear Lady Aberly addressing her daughter.

"You really must consider the advantages of marriage

to the Viscount. Do you want us to end up upon the street without a shilling? Do be realistic."

"I believe I have the interest of Mr. Ruyter. He will soon be a baron, Mama. I far prefer him to that dandy of a cousin."

Caroline heard Lady Aberly sigh. "As you wish, dear. I hope your headstrong notion does not lead us into despair."

Caroline gave a small cough before she entered. She had no desire to have her hostess guess that she had been listening. Still, she had every intention of trying to encourage Lavenia to add to her understanding of her strange relationship to Mr. Humphrey when they went to town on the morrow.

Lady Aberly pasted a smile over her previous look of anxiety. "Do join us, my dear. Lavenia and I were just speaking of how fatigued you must be to have slept so long."

Caroline nodded agreeably. "Traveling has taken more out of me than I realized."

Lavenia's expression clouded. "I trust you will be up to a trip to town tomorrow?"

Caroline nodded. "I would not miss the lovely temptation of Bath for any amount of rest."

"I fear you will not find Bath as exotic as India, though it does have its charm. I do not mean to make you homesick, but I have wondered how long your family has lived in India?" Lady Aberly said.

"My grandfather brought my father over as a little boy. But you are right, my lady. It does make me homesick to speak of them." Caroline was relieved to have found an excuse to avoid speaking of her invented family.

Lady Aberly smiled. "Of course. How thoughtless of me. I understand how you must miss them. We shall change the subject."

Lady Aberly listened indulgently as Lavenia burbled on about the wonders of Bath: the Sidney Gardens, the Pump Room, and Prior Park.

"Of course we shall have to sample Sally Lunn Buns. We shall bring some back for Mother. Have you ever tasted them?" Lavenia asked Caroline.

"No. I have not."

Lavenia beamed. "You have missed a rare treat. We shall have such a good time. I can hardly wait."

Lavenia's enthusiasm was catching. Caroline found her interest high as she rose in the morning and prepared for the trip. After Maggie finished buttoning the back of her day dress of pale blue jonquil muslin, Caroline hurried down to meet Lavenia.

She found her companion waiting eagerly. "John Coachman has already brought round the carriage. Maria will act as chaperon." She nodded to the servant who waited, expressionless, for the ladies to precede her from the house.

The trip to Bath intrigued Caroline, though she regretted trading the coveted view of the countryside for that of the city. Still, as they clattered across Pulteney Bridge to the center of town, Caroline found herself intrigued by the variety of shops.

They alighted at Milsom Street and entered the milliner's shop. "Perhaps I am mistaken, but I would think the bonnets here quite as nice as any in London," Lavenia commented.

Caroline glanced around at the variety of merchandise. She knew enough about such finery to agree with Lavenia. "They are remarkably in fashion. I have seen none finer on the streets of London."

Smiling from the assurance, Lavenia greeted the shop owner who scurried to attend them. "I would like to see the rose bonnet with the embroidered ribands."

The woman handed the bonnet to Lavenia. With delicately gloved hands, Lavenia placed it carefully on her head, then turned to view herself in the looking glass.

Biting her lip, she turned to Caroline. "What do you think? Perhaps I should try the straw bonnet with the primrose trim. I am so dreadfully short of day bonnets."

Caroline assured her that either choice went wonderfully well with her creamy complexion. Since she could not make a decision, Lavenia purchased both bonnets.

She handed the band boxes to her maid to place in the carriage while the young ladies continued their stroll toward George Street.

Caroline sought a means to bring up the subject that intrigued her. Perhaps Miss Lavenia would talk candidly now that she was out of her mother's hearing.

She sighed inwardly. Not "Miss" Lavenia, she reminded herself. She must learn to think of Lavenia as her equal if she were to succeed in the masquerade.

She spied a gentleman of refined attire entering a smoke shop. She touched Lavenia lightly on the arm. "I thought for a moment that gentleman was Lord Humphrey."

Lavenia met the statement with an unladylike scowl. "I should hope not. I would not like to meet that dandy on the street."

Caroline feigned surprise. However, the years she had spent overhearing the conversation of the gentry had taught her that private opinions did not always match public expression. The fact that Lavenia had not fully expressed her opinion of the Viscount during tea was obvious to Caroline.

Lavenia glanced behind them. She seemed assured that no one could overhear their conversation. "I should not tell you this, but since we are cousins, I shall. When Steffen's father gambled away the greater portion of their estate, Aunt Eleanor would have nothing to do with him. When Steffen followed in his father's gaming footsteps, Aunt Eleanor quite lost use for him also. I suppose he must stay in enough chips to keep himself in his fine clothes." Lavenia sniffed in an unladylike manner.

"He wishes to marry you?"

"He wishes to live at Castlegate Manor, I believe."

Caroline nodded. "I see. And what do you get out of the union?"

Lavenia flushed. "A title, I suppose."

Again, Caroline could not escape the feeling that she was holding something back.

They reached the bakery and Caroline lost herself in the delicious scent of fresh bread and rolls. Lavenia purchased an even dozen of Sally Lunn Buns and the young ladies nibbled on them as they watched the shoppers pass by. Never, Caroline thought, had any bread melted so delectably in her mouth.

They handed the remaining rolls to their attendant and continued their stroll down the street.

Lavenia pointed at an impressive stone building. "There is the theater where we shall attend the concert on Saturday."

Caroline swallowed hard. She knew nothing about such things. She would have to take careful clues from Lavenia. "I do hope I have an appropriate dress. I had little time to attend to garments while in London. I fear I may be a bit out of style." She hoped this explanation would cover the alterations she had done to Lady Eleanor's wardrobe.

Lavenia gave her a sweet smile. "I am sure you will look lovely in whatever you choose."

Caroline studied her companion. Lavenia had a kind face, devoid of the snobbery she had seen on so many. She liked the girl all the better the more she got to know her.

After stopping at a few more shops, they headed back to the carriage. "I shall have to hire a sedan chair if I walk any further," Lavenia proclaimed.

Caroline did not feel the least fatigued, but she waved her fan as vigorously as Lavenia in order to appear as delicate as any aristocrat.

As they neared the waiting carriage, a matronly woman stopped Lavenia. "My dear Miss Stewart. How delightful to see you here in Bath."

Lavenia curtesied. "Madam Ruyter. It is good to see you. May I introduce my cousin, Miss Caroline Stewart?"

Madam Ruyter nodded. "I trust you young ladies will

enjoy the upcoming concert. I know my Henry is quite looking forward to having you join our party."

"You are hospitable, my lady. My cousin and I will look forward to the event."

Caroline noted the flush on Lavenia's cheeks when the lady moved on. She was, no doubt, the mother of the young man who held Lavenia's interest. Lavenia's re-action bespoke a matter of the heart and not merely of convenience. For that, Caroline felt an unaccountable gladness. She wished the same for herself. Would she attain it?

Lavenia displayed high spirits on the ride back to Cas-tlegate Manor. "I do not know when I have so enjoyed a trip to the shops. I have always wanted a sister. Now, with you here, it is as though my wish has come true."

Caroline's conscience prickled at the deception that had enabled her to be a companion to Lavenia. Yet how nice it had been to speak as equals and be recognized by Madam Ruyter, obviously a respected member of the ton.

Saturday morning showers left a dampness that curled Caroline's wavy hair into wisps about her face. Tonight, she would attire herself as a lady and accompany Lady Aberly and Lavenia to the theater.

A persistent anxiety wedged itself in her heart as she stared into her looking glass. Without resorting to vanity, she knew that she was appealing. Her heart-shaped face contained wide dark eyes fringed with long lashes, a well-shaped nose and generous lips. It was not the face that bothered her. Instead, it was the unnerving feeling that she was looking at a stranger.

A servant's uniform topped with a white starched bonnet should have greeted her. The woman in the mirror wore a day dress of soft rose mull. White gloved fingers tied a straw bonnet with matching rose ribands in place. Yes, the face was right. But the apparel all wrong.

She rose briskly from the dressing table. She must not give attention to these doubts. Like a fairy godmother, Lady Eleanor wished to give her this chance to become a lady. She would not be so foolish as to allow her childish insecurity to spoil it.

By afternoon tea, a sense of preparation permeated the entire household. Servants scurried to bring starched petticoats and polished slippers.

After a short rest, the ladies began the task of dressing for the evening outing. Caroline had made a careful study of her gowns. After consulting Lavenia, she chose a soft turquoise gown of sheer jaconet.

As she joined the other ladies for a light supper, she admired Lavenia's high-cheeked beauty. She wondered about Mr. Henry Ruyter and what sort of man he might be. From Lavenia's flushed cheeks, Caroline could only suppose he was as dashing as Lavenia was lovely.

As they were helped into the carriage, Lady Aberly seemed in a nervous jitter. "Lavenia, I do not believe that bonnet goes best with your features. I do wish you had chosen one with a thinner brim."

Lavenia slid beside her mother. "Then I would have no excuse to tilt up my face to bat my eyes at Mr. Ruyter."

The older lady clucked her disapproval. "Do not be vulgar. If he does not declare his intentions soon, I shall have to insist you accept betrothal to your cousin."

As Lavenia caught her lip, Caroline felt annoyance at Lady Aberly's persistent badgering. Surely, it was not necessary for Lavenia to rush into marriage with anyone. She seemed most comfortably ensconced at Castlegate Manor and she did have prospects for a suitable match.

Again, Caroline had the feeling that there was something about the situation of these ladies that was quite outside her knowledge. But at the present, the prospect of conducting herself properly at the upcoming event drove these thoughts from her mind.

Chapter Three

Caroline offered a delicate, gloved hand to the footman as she alighted from the carriage to the grandeur of the theater rising before her. Inside, as she became surrounded by splendidly clad patrons, the enormity of her pretense threatened to suffocate her.

She took a deep breath and followed Lady Aberly and Lavenia to the foot of the stairs, where she recognized Madam Ruyter and a young man she supposed was Henry.

She forgot herself as she attended to the introductions. Henry looked nothing as she expected. Tall and thin, his features somewhat sharp and his hands overly large for his wrists, he was not the dashing prince she had pictured for Lavenia. And yet, a glance at Lavenia's enraptured face told Caroline that Lavenia imagined him the most winsome man alive.

They proceeded up to the boxes where a baron and baroness of Mrs. Ruyter's acquaintance were already seated. The older couple greeted them amiably as they took seats in the comfortably padded chairs, Lavenia beside Henry and Caroline beside Lady Aberly.

As she awaited the performance, Caroline took note of the fine surroundings. Rich velvet curtains of ruby red were secured by ties at either side of all the boxes. Below, the stage was curtained with the same rich velvet.

Lady Aberly leaned to explain, "I believe our soprano will be performing a series of baroque arias."

Caroline nodded and tried to pretend she had understood. Relief possessed her as the curtain rose, relieving her of the need to reply.

Lady Aberly raised her spy glass to view the finely attired woman who appeared on stage, while the Baron and Baroness took turns sleeping through the first half of the performance.

When the intermission came, Mrs. Ruyter remained with the Baron and Baroness while Lady Aberly accompanied the younger folk for a breath of air and a glass of lemonade.

As Henry and Lavenia stopped to chat with another couple, Caroline became aware of a man approaching them through the crowd. She felt a sudden dread as Lord Steffen Humphrey approached.

He took her hand and bowed. "Good evening, cousin. You are looking particularly fetching this evening. I believe that bonnet brings out the amber in your eyes."

She withdrew her hand as soon as she dared. "Viscount. How kind of you to notice me." What was it about the man she did not trust?

He nodded curtly in Lavenia's direction. "I see my

competitor has won the heart of my other fair cousin. I warn you, I do not intend to let you get away."

Though said lightly, the words sent a chill through Caroline's body. "I should rejoin my party, sir."

"Of course. I shall look forward to our next encounter."

With another bow, he departed.

The intermission ended and the small party made their way back to the box. Caroline fanned herself steadily as the closeness of the theater made her feel like steamed pudding. Though the lovely voice of the soprano captured her interest, she was glad when the performance ended and she could escape into the relative coolness of night.

The coach took them over cobblestone streets to the residence of Madam Ruyter. A small party had gathered in the salon by the time they arrived, including two young men whose acquaintance she had not made. Caroline scanned the room and did not see Lord Humphrey. For that, she breathed a sigh of relief.

Lavenia drew her to the group of young people. "Caroline, these are two of Mr. Ruyter's friends, Mr. Arnold and Mr. Blois. Gentlemen, this is my cousin, Miss Caroline Stewart. She has recently come from London to visit us."

The young men bowed.

Mr. Blois smiled, showing perfect white teeth. "I am pleased to meet you, Miss Stewart. Do you reside in London?"

She shook her head, pleased to see the admiring looks

from the two young men. "No. I have come to the country to stay with my aunt, Lady Aberly."

"You must miss London," said Mr. Arnold, his interest showing in his round countenance.

Caroline's thoughts drifted unbidden to her childhood and the parents whom she still missed. "Yes. I do miss it."

A strange look from Lavenia brought her suddenly alert. At no time must she allow herself to forget her story. "Of course I was not there long enough to become truly attached. You see, my great-aunt died shortly after I arrived."

Mr. Blois affixed himself at her elbow. "Arrived from where?"

She caught her lip. The lie seemed harder to tell. "From India." She sincerely hoped no one would question her about the weather, wildlife, or scenery.

Mr. Arnold positioned himself at her other elbow. "How fascinating. You must tell more about it."

"Perhaps when I have sampled some punch. I am quite parched from the ride here."

"Of course. I shall fetch it," Mr. Blois offered eagerly.

Caroline allowed herself to be seated on a salon sofa with Mr. Arnold. Across the room, she spotted Lavenia and Henry seated together. When Mr. Blois returned, Caroline steered the conversation to topics regarding what the two gentlemen did with their time. The fact that there was no more talk of India relieved her greatly.

She studied the two men with an eye toward a husband. Mr. Arnold was as round-faced as a schoolboy and had an annoying habit of touching her sleeve.

Mr. Blois was decidedly more handsome, yet had a way of droning on about his affairs that put Caroline nearly to sleep.

When the evening ended, Caroline was grateful to follow her party to the coach. Both gentlemen bid her a fond good-bye with the promise to seek her out at future social functions.

Inside the coach, Lady Aberly asked, "Did you have a good time, my dears?"

Caroline nodded. "I could not have asked for more attentive company than the two gentlemen who were introduced to me."

Lady Aberly frowned. "You can likely do better. Neither of those young men have the social position of my Lavenia's Henry. Perhaps we should host a party. Caroline would meet more of the haut ton."

She turned to Lavenia. "You would like a party, would you not, dear? Perhaps we will have something to announce.

Lavenia flushed. "I would like that, Mama."

Caroline felt sorry for the girl. It seemed Lady Aberly was pressing ever harder for the assurance that Mr. Ruyter was about to make his declaration. Caroline was sure Lavenia would be only too happy to share the news as soon as things were settled.

They rode in relative silence, each caught in her own thoughts. Caroline was surprised to see a carriage waiting at the door when they arrived at this late hour.

Lady Aberly wrung her fine lace handkerchief. "Oh dear. I do fear I know who has come to call. What shall I tell him, Lavenia?"

"Make an excuse, any excuse. I shall not marry him no matter what happens with Henry."

Fearing to intrude, Caroline kept quiet as the footman handed them down. At the door, Edwards announced the guest who waited in the parlor.

"Lord Humphrey is here to see you, Madam."

Lady Aberly motioned the young ladies to hasten upstairs, but Lord Humphrey appeared before they could make their escape. "I see you have been out to a party to which I was not invited." His voice sounded slurred.

Lady Aberly nodded. "We were invited to the home of Madam Ruyter."

He winked at Lavenia. "I see. I should be jealous, you know. In fact, a duel would not be out of order, except for the arrival of this exquisite creature." He nodded to Caroline.

She felt her knees grow weak, yet determination kept her gaze level as she met his eyes. She refused to show him any sign of weakness, not when he was in a superior position to force her into marriage.

He swayed slightly. "I will be master of Castlegate Manor. I know the old lady left it to you, but it rightfully belongs to me."

Lady Aberly waved her fan vigorously. "You are in your cups, Steffen, and you do not know what you are saying. I shall have your man help you into your coach."

Lord Humphrey fell silent, not resisting as his man assisted him out the door. When he was safely away, Lady Aberly collapsed into a chair. "No doubt he was here much of the evening, drinking himself into that state. I shall be glad when you are married to your

Henry, Lavenia, though I do not know where that should leave me."

Lavenia patted her mother's shoulder. "You will always be welcome with us, Mama."

Lady Aberly eyed Caroline wearily. "That will leave you to deal with Lord Humphrey as you choose. Perhaps a wedding would not be a bad solution."

Caroline could think of no reply. She felt as though she were being bartered in place of Lavenia. If a maiden offering were to be made, she was not at all sure she wished it to be herself.

She had come expecting to weigh the allure of true love against the security of money and a social position. She had thought she could choose security. Surely she would have security if she married into this household.

But why did Lady Aberly expect she would have no place here should Lavenia marry Mr. Ruyter? Had not Lady Aberly inherited this estate?

Again, she was plagued with the feeling that there were more questions than answers where Lady Aberly and Lavenia were concerned. Considering the late hour of the night and the pounding at her temples, she decided any more speculation would have to wait until the morning.

She crawled into bed and was immediately asleep.

Upon awakening, the call of the moorhens reminded Caroline that she was in the country. Before she left London, she had found security in the sounds there. The calls of the fish sellers in the market square were familiar to her servant ears. Now that she had traded that position for a country miss, she knew she longed to stay here with all her heart.

She stood at the window and looked across the verdant fields. Her eyes fell on the stables where the grooms were at work exercising the horses. She had always had a fascination with the beasts. When she was a very small girl, Tom Coachman had sometimes unhitched the carriage horses and put her on the back of a gentle horse named Bob.

She remembered those days with fondness. Perhaps a trip to the stable would help assuage the anxiety last evening had caused. Since Lady Aberly and Lavenia were late sleepers, it would be easy to slip away unnoticed after breakfast.

Caroline dressed in pale blue muslin and pulled her hair up in a simple style under a sensible straw bonnet. Feeling that she was properly attired for an after-breakfast walk to the stable, she ate a quick repast in the parlor and slipped out the door.

She passed under the giant hornbeams, their leaves casting a trail of shade as she walked the path to the stable. The sounds of nickering and the male voices that answered in soothing tones filled her with an unexplainable excitement.

Her eyes were on the corral and the handsome roan when she stumbled against the young stable hand as she rounded the corner of the building. In a crash of bodies, Caroline found herself off balance, tumbling toward a broad chest. Then, strong arms caught her in a firm grip and set her back on her feet.

She looked up into the darkest green eyes she had ever seen and felt her heart skip a beat.

"I am begging your pardon, sir," she muttered. Then remembering her position, she blushed furiously. What was she thinking, apologizing to a stable hand? She was glad Lady Aberly had not witnessed the scene.

A smile played at the corner of his well-formed lips. "It was my fault, my lady. Have you been injured?"

Caroline shook her head, still flustered from the physical nature of their encounter. "I am fine. I fear I was admiring that fine horse instead of watching where I was going."

She noticed that he watched her with interest as she righted her bonnet. Her annoyance with herself grew with the realization that she was enjoying his attention. If she had any hope of her scheme succeeding, she must remember her position.

She forced herself to regain the composure that had been shattered in the encounter. "I am Miss Stewart, newly arrived from London to stay with my aunt. I had hoped to see some of the horses."

He tilted an eyebrow in a gesture that was almost patronizing. "Really? It is nice to meet you, my lady. I am Geoffrey, newly arrived at the stables."

As he stood staring at her, she saw an amused light in his eyes. His chestnut hair shimmered in the early sunlight. Taking herself in hand, Caroline tried again to become mistress of the situation.

"Would you be so kind as to walk me through the stables, Geoffrey?"

Geoffrey gave a slight bow. "As you wish, my lady."

He followed as she rounded the building to the rows of stalls that held only a dozen horses. Caroline wondered if a former master of the estate had enjoyed hunting parties. With only the three ladies in the house, the use of horses was reserved primarily for carriage rides.

An older man looked up from examining a hoof as Caroline strolled past the stalls.

"Miss Stewart has come to admire the horses," Geoffrey told the ostler.

The man tipped his hat. "Morning, ma'm. If you decide to ride, Geoffrey can saddle a horse for you and your abigail."

Caroline did not want to admit she had abandoned propriety and come alone. "I am not dressed for riding. Perhaps I shall come back another time."

The man nodded and continued his duty with the horse.

Back in the sunshine, Caroline strolled to the corral. The lovely roan nickered and shook his mane as she paused to study him. "What a lovely horse. What is his name?"

"Victory. He is named for Lord Nelson's flagship."

"How interesting. Where did Lady Aberly get him?"

"She did not buy him, Miss. He is mine. I rode him here."

Caroline studied the groom briefly as his startling green eyes rested fondly on his horse. Caroline knew little about horses, but she could tell the animal in the corral was of fine quality.

"Where did you get him?"

"I won him in a bet, but I do not suppose such things are of interest to a lady like yourself."

Caroline found herself flushing even as she wondered where he got the money for such a bet. He was an unusual man, especially for a groom. She had lived her life with servants. In comparison, this young man's forward manner and lack of humility disturbed her. Even more disturbing was the way her pulse behaved ever since she had run into him.

Caroline decided she should return to the house. It would not be advisable for her to be seen keeping company with this man.

She nodded curtly. "I thank you for showing me the horses. Now I shall be going."

Geoffrey bowed. "I do hope you will come back for a ride. I would be happy to escort you and your abigail, and perhaps Miss Lavenia."

Caroline felt a twinge of jealousy. "Does Miss Lavenia come riding?"

"I would not know, Miss. I have only just arrived."

Caroline bit her lip. "I fear I am a poor rider. There was not much occasion in London."

Geoffrey's smile spread across his smooth features. "Of course, Miss. I should be happy to teach you anything you need to know."

The statement sounded slightly teasing, but Caroline had no proof of his intent. She responded somewhat tartly. "Perhaps I shall ride on another day. Good-day, Geoffrey."

"Good-day, Miss."

His deep voice seemed to hover in the air behind her

as she turned for the house. Something about this man disrupted her composure. She would have to be careful to keep the proper distance between them.

She arrived at the house to find Lady Aberly and Lavenia at breakfast. "I could hardly sleep a wink last night after that dreadful visit by Mr. Humphrey," Lady Aberly admitted.

Lavenia turned to Caroline. "What do you think of him?"

Caroline tore her thoughts from the groom to Lord Humphrey, who seemed quite the fop by comparison.

"He dresses very well," she answered mildly.

Lady Aberly fanned herself. "He has not always been the way he behaved last night. I hear he has had some financial setbacks of late."

Caroline accepted the invitation to seat herself beside Lavenia. The maid brought an extra cup and Caroline accepted tea from Lady Aberly.

Lavenia nibbled a sweet cake. "He fancies the estate. I think he is not pleased that no immediate plans have formed to bring him here."

Caroline swallowed hard and wondered if he were a violent man. What wrath would she incur if she were to marry him, only to have him find out her true station? She could never take that chance. Her safety lay in marrying someone outside the Stewart family. Unfortunately, she could not convey this knowledge to any of the parties involved.

Talk turned to other matters, particularly the party that Lady Aberly had proposed. Lavenia bloomed with the possibility of dressing for her Henry and dancing away an entire evening.

There was much planning to do and invitations to write. Caroline had little to offer except her willingness to help wherever needed.

Lady Aberly patted her arm. "You just take care for your frock. I am sure we can manage the rest."

Just before lunch a carriage arrived. Caroline's heart sank as she heard Lord Humphrey speaking to Edwards in the front hall.

Lady Aberly floated out, determined to behave as a gracious hostess despite her personal feelings. "Why Lord Humphrey, how kind of you to drop by. Perhaps you will stay for lunch?"

He engaged her with a smile. "I would be honored. I have come to apologize for my beastly behavior last night. I must admit, I hardly remember what was said or done."

Lady Aberly nodded politely. "I am sure you were not yourself. We will not speak of it again. I shall ring for Maggie to tell Cook to prepare an extra dinner."

Mr. Humphrey turned to the young women. "I would like a word with Miss Caroline. Perhaps Maggie would be so kind as to bring some handwork to the garden and complete it out of hearing."

He turned to Lady Aberly. "I assure you there will be no untoward behavior on my part."

Lady Aberly's anxious look at Caroline belied her mild answer. "I am sure that would be acceptable to our guest."

Trapped like a mouse, Caroline desperately reviewed

her choices. She clutched the back of the armchair. "I fear I am unwell, my lord. The theater last night tired me more than I expected. Perhaps you would excuse me and we might have our talk another time."

Lord Humphrey's dark features hardened in irritation. However, his station required that his manners respect a lady's delicate constitution.

"As you wish. I shall take my leave and trust you will feel better on my next visit."

"I am sure I shall."

Caroline excused herself to her room, feeling a missed lunch a small price to pay to escape from the overbearing Viscount.

Chapter Four

In Lady Aberly's enthusiasm, the plans for the upcoming party quickly expanded. The guest list grew as did the need for elaborate preparations. Caroline began to feel rather lost as Lavenia and her mother went about their days in planning for the occasion.

On one such day, Caroline looked out to the stables and found she had a clear view of Geoffrey grooming the beautiful roan horse. Unable to deny her impulse, she decided to see what he could teach her about riding.

His servant status would preclude him from ever telling anyone of influence about any faux pas she might make in her efforts as a horsewoman. And, perhaps, she might ride the roan that she found worthy of admiration.

She broached the need for a riding habit with Lavenia. "I had no need for such attire either in India or London. I shall endeavor to acquire my own outfit on our next trip into Bath. However, I've taken it into my head to

41

go for a ride and wondered if you might have something you could loan me for today."

"Of course."

Lavenia found a dark green velvet riding outfit with a matching top hat and veil. Caroline tried it on in the privacy of her room. She stood in front of her looking glass and twirled the full skirt. She found it fit her suitably well. The color went well with her dark hair and eyes and the skirt pinched in about her slim waist.

She gathered her borrowed riding crop and, followed by the abigail Lavenia had lent for the morning, made her way down the path to the stable. She had been pleased, that in her distraction with the party, Lavenia had shown no interest in joining in the ride.

Her pulse quickened as she spied Geoffrey pitching hay for the stable horses into the corral. For a brief moment, she allowed herself to wonder whether it was the horses or the groom that had really drawn her attention. She put the thought from her mind as she addressed the tall young groom.

"I've come for a ride. Would you be so kind as to saddle a horse? I'm afraid I shall need advice and assistance. It has been some time since I have been for a ride."

"I would be most happy to assist you," Geoffrey answered, agreeably securing a plump mare from the corral.

Caroline caught her lip between her teeth. "I had hoped at some point I might ride Victory."

He studied her for a moment and Caroline flushed under his candid gaze. "At some point, perhaps. But Victory is a spirited horse for a beginner. I fear you might have difficulty controlling him."

His words seemed to carry an implication that Caroline was unable to discern. "Then I shall accept your advice as to my mount."

Caroline waited in the shade of the path while Geoffrey chose another mare for the abigail and led the horses to be properly saddled.

An altercation in the stable caught Caroline's attention. An unfamiliar male voice was raised in argument with the old ostler Caroline had met on her first visit to the stable.

After a moment, Geoffrey emerged, seeming unruffled.

She frowned. "Pray, tell me, what that was all about."

Geoffrey held her mount and lifted her into the saddle. Caroline felt her skin tingle at his touch. He had lifted her without effort, as though she were as tiny as a child.

Then, peering up to answer, he said, "Mr. Humphrey has employed another groom. He felt we were understaffed even with my arrival. I think he would like to rebuild the stable to its former grandeur should he ever be lord here."

"But the argument?" Caroline persisted.

"The new groom wished to accompany you. However, as we had already settled that arrangement, it required our boss to set things straight."

"I see."

Caroline felt flattered to be the object of interest, even if the two men were below her supposed status.

She held her head high as Geoffrey mounted Victory

and, followed by the abigail, they began a sedate walk down the shaded dirt path to the grassland beyond.

When they reached the gently rolling land, Geoffrey turned to say, "I believe we might safely increase your pace to a canter, if you like, Miss. Old Beauty there has a gentle gait."

Caroline laughed. "Beauty, is it? Well, perhaps in her youth."

The fresh air had a relaxing effect, unlike the mounting excitement inside the house. She studied Geoffrey under her lashes as he rode along beside her. His speech was proper for that of a groom. He had obviously not gone without education.

"I shall trust you to set the pace," she directed.

Geoffrey urged Victory into a gentle canter. Caroline kept pace while the abigail trotted behind.

Here was a man with whom she might have enjoyed keeping company had she come here as a servant. How ironic that, because of her own lie, she would never know if the attraction she felt was genuine. How many fine men might there be who were now below her station?

Her musings were cut short when a loud gunshot tore the peaceful glen. Caroline felt Beauty give a violent lurch before breaking into a terrified run. With no time to consider what had gone wrong, Caroline spent her energy trying to hang onto the frightened creature.

Hooves pounded behind her and she knew, without looking, that Geoffrey was in hot pursuit. Even in her terror, she felt an unreasoning assurance that he would be able to save her and stop the runaway mare.

She could see him beside her. He reached for her reins just as her horse stumbled. The lurch sent Caroline out of the saddle to tumble onto a grassy knoll.

The reassuring thought that he would still save her was her last memory before she felt the wind knocked from her body and a darkness block all consciousness.

Geoffrey pulled the frightened horses to a halt and sprang from his saddle. Caroline lay crumpled on the ground. He rolled her over gently, his heart in his throat at the sight of her pale face. Her lashes fell in a dark fan on her ivory cheeks.

At that moment, though he had known her only a short time, Geoffrey knew without a doubt that he truly admired her. For the first time, he had found a woman who honestly intrigued him. It seemed a cruel twist of fate that she might be stolen from him just as he recognized how much he wished to know her better.

Above the lace of her habit shirt, he spied the faint pulse that still beat in her slender neck. She roused, opening her eyes, and he knew he had been holding his breath. She stared at him vacantly, then struggled to sit up.

"Not too fast," he cautioned. "You took a nasty fall."

He placed an arm behind her slender back and cradled her against his chest. "Are you in pain?"

She lay against him, trying to regain her sense of balance. He knew, like a common cad, he was taking advantage of her weakened condition. Still, he was drawn to the lavender scent of her hair, the sweet softness of her body. He felt quite loath to let her go.

She struggled in his arms. "I do not believe that I have broken any bones."

"Then you are likely just bruised and shaken."

"Perhaps if you would help me to my feet, I could be sure of my situation."

He longed to ignore her protest, sweep her into his arms, and carry her back to the estate. Instead, he would remember his position. He must, he thought wryly. It would be awkward for the old ostler, Carter, if she were to demand Geoffrey's dismissal. He had no choice but to play his part.

He released her and lifted her gently to her feet.

The abigail trotted up. "Are you alright, Miss? I seen the horse take off and you hanging on for dear life. Please tell me you 'aven't broke any bones."

Caroline smiled shakily. "I believe only my dignity has been harmed."

She stared up at Geoffrey with a frown. "What was that noise I heard just before Beauty bolted?"

"It was a gunshot, Miss. No doubt a poacher was hunting rabbit."

"Oh."

Caroline seemed satisfied with his answer as she brushed grass from her riding skirt. Geoffrey did not believe for a moment it had been a poacher hiding in the bushes. The bullet had likely been meant for him. If so, it would mean he had been found out. He would have to be watchful as he proceeded with his plan.

Caroline straightened her habit. "Does it happen often, this poaching, I mean?"

Geoffrey stared at her full lips that were filled again

with color and he longed to taste their sweetness. Forcing himself to meet her eyes he said, "I don't think it has ever happened before. I shouldn't worry about it."

"Is it safe to go back now?"

Geoffrey glanced back to the woods that had concealed their assailant. "I am sure whoever frightened the horses has taken his rabbit and left the woods. However, we will stay far to this side. I am sure we will be quite safe."

He lifted Caroline easily onto her horse, pleased to note that she did not refuse to get back in the saddle. He could not abide women who became hysterical at the slightest provocation. Caroline had a practicality that he found immensely appealing.

They walked the horses back to the stable so as not to jar Caroline's already bruised person. Except for the fall, she had found the mad pelt across the meadow somewhat exhilarating. Her pulse still raced when she remembered Geoffrey riding hard in pursuit. She had regained consciousness in the warmth of his arms. The security she had felt had been nearly worth the fall.

She glanced beside her to see him riding erect and self-assured in the saddle. His handsome features and confident bearing could pass him off as an aristocrat. If only he could trade places with that annoying Mr. Humphrey. She would welcome the attentions of Geoffrey as much as she disliked the attention of the Viscount.

She sighed and scolded herself for such silly thoughts. The penchant she had for engaging in fantasies did her no good. Life was what it was and she would have to live with it. She could not encourage Geoffrey, but neither did she have to give up her riding. She did quite enjoy the sport and, if his company came with it, that was no fault of her own.

At the stables, Geoffrey helped her from her horse. Concern showed in his eyes. "Are you sure you were not injured?"

She smiled into the green inquiry of his gaze. "I am sure. I am also sure that my accident has not put me off of riding. I will keep trying until I learn to sit a horse."

"You did well to stay on as long as you did. You have the making of a fine horsewoman, my lady."

His kind words hung in her mind as she and the abigail walked the path to the house. She went into the parlor to find Lady Aberly and Lavenia having a late breakfast.

Lady Aberly frowned. "You look a bit rumpled, my dear. I trust you had no trouble with your ride."

Caroline cast a warning glance at the abigail and replied mildly, "The ride was quite invigorating. However, I believe the jaunt in the wind has left me disheveled. If you will excuse me, I shall retire to my room for repairs."

Once sequestered in her quarters, Caroline allowed the chambermaid to help her out of the riding habit and into a day dress of rose muslin. She set the top hat carefully back into the box and surveyed her tousled hair.

Maggie took up a brush and began to smooth the chestnut tangles. Her eyes widened at the bits of grass that fell onto the dressing table. Caroline expected her thoughts had taken a turn in the wrong direction. She did not want to be the subject of the upstairs servants' speculation, even until Lavenia's abigail could put things right.

"I took a fall while riding. I do not wish my aunt to know of the incident. It would only worry her."

Caroline could still see a dozen questions in Maggie's eyes. Fortunately, propriety would keep her from asking.

In short order, her hair was restored to fashion, tied with rose ribbons at the side, and falling in a gentle wave down her back. She studied her reflection with approval. If only she could keep from doing any more unladylike things, such as falling off a horse. She felt sure that Lady Eleanor, if she were still alive, would not have approved of her afternoon adventure.

Now, she would engage in an activity she was sure Lady Eleanor would have approved of. She had been longing to peruse the well-stocked library. Several years ago, Lady Eleanor had insisted that Caroline learn to read. She patiently instructed the young girl. In return, in the dear lady's declining years, the stories Caroline read aloud each day provided her with a source of pleasure and amusement.

Reluctantly, Caroline had Maggie return the borrowed riding habit to Lavenia's room. Lavenia had planned a trip to Bath for material for new gowns. While there, Caroline could choose a velvet for a riding garment for herself. Then, she could go riding every morning if she wished. After all, if she were to become the wife of a country squire, she would have to learn to play the part.

On the way past the parlor, Caroline heard a male voice.

She paused in curiosity. Catching sight of her, Lavenia

drew her into the room. "Why, Caroline, Mr. Blois has come to call. I have persuaded him to join us for us a meal."

Caroline fought her disappointment with her change of plans for inspecting the library and reminded herself that she must choose a husband before her role as impostor was discovered. Perhaps she had been tired on the night of Lady Ruyter's party and not given Mr. Blois a fair chance.

As they sat for their light repast, she nearly laughed aloud at the silliness of herself, a servant girl, feeling she could be so particular with a husband. What would Mr. Blois, or any of the other young men, think if they knew the truth about her?

All through the meal, he spoke about his latest activities working with the solicitor. Caroline found her mind wandering and, with great effort, remembered to favor him with an occasional nod and smile. As they lingered over a cup of tea, he laced and unlaced his long fingers in a gesture Caroline found quite distracting.

It was with private relief that Caroline bid him good afternoon when he proclaimed his need to return to the city. He took her hand and bent over it most gallantly. "You will save room on your dance card for me at your aunt's party, will you not?"

Caroline felt her pulse quicken with alarm. Lady Eleanor had taught her to read, but Caroline had never had occasion to learn to dance. That she would be expected to do so at the ball had not entered her mind.

She forced a smile. "I shall, my lord."

She watched his retreating figure and knew she had no intention of keeping her promise.

Finally, she was free to escape to her private passion. Books would ask nothing of her. They would not accidentally uncover her masquerade. In the library, she would be free to lose herself in the concerns of fictional characters and forget her own subterfuge. Here, she would be safe.

She turned the knob of the library door and pushed it open, ignoring its protesting creak. On the far wall, the French doors stood open, letting in a fresh breeze from the garden. Caroline could see Robert, the gardener, tending roses. The lovely perfume of the blossoms filled the air.

Though the servants kept the room dusted, Caroline did not think that either Lady Aberly or Lavenia used it often. Though Lavenia had spoken of Jane Austen, she had admitted that she had yet to read any of her work.

Caroline had read it to Lady Eleanor and they had both liked it immensely. Perhaps, she would find other volumes among the many rows of books which would also catch her fancy.

She stood before a stack of books and read the titles. The musty smell of the older volumes reminded her of Lady Eleanor's library in London.

She spotted a volume of Fanny Burney's *Evelina*, and had just plucked it from the shelf when a voice beside the open French doors startled her. The book tumbled from her fingers as she turned to see Lord Humphrey framed in the doorway. A smug smile spread across his thin lips as he observed her discomposure.

"My dear Miss Stewart, I did not mean to startle you. I wish to have a word with you if you are not too occupied."

He crossed to retrieve the fallen book. Caroline shrank from his nearness as he seemed to deliberately brush against her as he straightened to hand her the book.

"Thank you, my lord. Perhaps you would like to sit. I could order tea, or coffee if you would prefer."

She glanced toward the hallway, uncomfortable at being alone with him and eager to rectify the situation. Lord Humphrey, however, seemed intent upon a personal conference.

"I require nothing expect to sit with you and finish our talk. Perhaps we could sit in those chairs beside the fireplace."

Caroline proceeded to the chairs which faced the cold hearth. In the winter, the setting might have engendered a homey warmth. On this summer day, with the Viscount beside her, Caroline felt no comfort in either the location or position in which she found herself.

He turned to face her. "My dear Miss Stewart, my regard for you has not escaped your attention. I do not wish to press my suit upon you, but I see no reason for delay when we are obviously suited to one another."

Caroline stared at her trembling hands. "Really, my lord, we hardly know one another."

"I know all I need know about you."

Caroline's heart skipped a beat in reflex to her guilty secret. She relaxed as he continued.

"You are a lady of breeding and beauty. I have a title to offer. Have we need of more?"

Caroline stifled the urge to laugh at his description of her background. "Yes, my lord, I would need to know a great deal more about you to consider marriage."

His expression darkened. "You had a bit of a riding accident this morning, did you not?"

"How did you know about that?"

"The new groom I employed supplied the information."

Caroline caught her lip, confused by the turn of conversation.

Lord Humphrey continued to lean forward. "Consider this, Miss Stewart. I always get what I want. And I want you. There could be other uncomfortable happenings in this household, if you prove obstinate to my suit."

Caroline caught her breath. "What did you have to do with what happened this morning?"

The Viscount studied his immaculate nails. He smiled an unpleasant smile that did not reach his eyes. "Perhaps nothing."

Caroline clasped her fingers to control their trembling. "I will not be threatened into marriage, sir."

Their eyes locked in a battle of will. Lord Humphrey's eyes narrowed. "We shall see."

He stood and gave a small bow.

Caroline looked away in dismissal. She sensed the Viscount's gaze resting upon her.

"I understand your aunt is giving a ball. I hope our little dispute does not disincline you from allowing me to sign your dance card."

Caroline replied without favoring him with a glance. "I shall not be rude, my lord."

"Good. I shall look forward to our next meeting. In the meantime, please consider what I have said."

As he left the room, Caroline found her thoughts in turmoil. Foremost in her mind was the knowledge that Geoffrey worked in the stable. Had he anything to do with the plot to marry her to Lord Humphrey? If so, proof of his treachery would cause her more pain than the acts themselves.

She needed someone to trust. Yet, who would that be? No one knew her true circumstances.

She decided on the only course open to her. She would share as much as she could with her aunt and Lavenia during tea and hope they could provide counsel.

Chapter Five

Caroline accepted her tea with the hope that the turmoil which churned within her did not show on her face. While Lady Aberly talked on about the ball, Caroline could not keep her thoughts on a word that was spoken. At last Lady Aberly said, "You seem distracted, my dear. Whatever is on your mind?"

This provided just the opening for which Caroline was hoping. She set down her cup and composed her countenance.

"I had a visit with Lord Humphrey in the library. It was most troublesome."

Lady Aberly frowned. "Was it? Why was that?"

Caroline did not wish to alarm the ladies, but she did want to give fair warning in case Lord Humphrey's evil schemes affected them as well as herself.

"He said that we would find life uncomfortable here if I did not agree to marry him."

Lavenia gave a startled gasp. "How horrible! Whatever could he mean by that?"

Caroline was loath to reveal the riding mishap for fear her aunt would forbid her from returning to the stable. "He hinted that a mischief would come to us, an accident perhaps."

Lavenia's lips parted in astonishment.

Lady Aberly clicked her tongue. "Oh, la. I think you must be making more of it than is wont by the circumstances. You must have misunderstood. Lord Humphrey can be tedious when he is in his cups, but I do not believe he would do anything to harm us."

Caroline would not presume to disagree with Lady Aberly, so she took a different approach. "Perhaps you would help me understand why he wishes to rush into marriage. We have not known each other long enough to develop a true attachment."

Lavenia set aside her cup of tea. "Perhaps he believes that it is his only way to gain control of Castlegate Manor. He must believe that you will inherit it. He wishes to marry you before another suitor claims you and takes his place."

Caroline frowned. "But I have inherited nothing. Does he not see you and your mother living here after Lady Eleanor's death? Surely he knows you are the heirs. It is you he should still wish to wed."

Lady Aberly appeared flustered. "I suppose he got the idea from me. You must not tell him about your lack of the inheritance. Please, if you speak now, he may bring trouble about Lavenia's wedding. After the wedding, simply tell him the truth."

Caroline caught her lip. What was the truth? It was getting harder for her to imagine.

"Of course I shall say nothing. I would not do anything to disturb the wedding of two people who are so obviously in love."

Lavenia placed her hand atop Caroline's. Her eyes shone with emotion. "You are truly like a sister to me."

Caroline smiled. "I am an only child, too. Like you, I have always wanted a sister."

It felt good to share a little of her past. She *was* an only child; that much was the truth.

Lady Aberly seemed pleased that the unpleasant conversation had come to an end. For her part, Caroline tried to ignore the resentment she felt toward the older woman. Lady Aberly had put her in an awkward and perhaps dangerous position in order to free her own daughter to marry. The best that could be done now was to stall Lord Humphrey until after Lavenia's wedding. Then Caroline could tell him that it was Lady Aberly and her daughter who had inherited this lovely estate— in entirety—and not herself.

The next morning, they arose early for a light repast. Each lady eagerly anticipated the trip to Bath to visit the famous salon of Madam Marian. There they would choose the material she would use to create their gowns.

Caroline felt a mixture of excitement and anxiety. She had gone with Lady Eleanor on several occasions to choose material for new ball gowns. Yet, she had never chosen one for herself.

She must choose well and make a good impression.

The ball might be her chance to meet a suitable match. She could not afford to come ill-attired.

Fortunately, Lavenia misunderstood her anxiety. "You must not worry. Madam Marian is the best dressmaker in all of Bath. She will produce a perfect fit."

Caroline smiled. "I am sure she will."

John Coachman brought the carriage round and the old groom, Nottington, helped the ladies inside. Despite her careful preparations, Caroline keenly felt her pretense of being a lady.

She silently chastised herself with the fact that, if she talked and dressed like a lady, no one would know the fears and insecurities that plagued her existence. She would simply have to be careful at Madam Marian's and do exactly as Lady Aberly and Lavenia did.

They talked of fabrics and fashions and what had been popular in London as they clattered from the estate onto the road that led to Bath.

"My, but this is a most bumpy ride. I wonder if the rains last night have done damage to the road," Lavenia complained.

Caroline was inclined to agree. She had not remembered this road being so bad on their previous trip to Bath.

However, Lady Aberly, not wishing to abandon her favorite topic of fashion and fabric, dismissed the jolting with a flounce of her curls. "I dare say we will be past the worst part soon."

Suddenly the carriage gave a massive lurch which sent the three ladies tumbling together into a colorful pile of skirts and bonnets. They tilted sideways as the broken carriage came to rest with a powerful thud.

The moment of silence following the violent rasping and jolting gave Caroline a chance to take stock of her circumstances. The ladies rested against the side of the carriage with poor Lady Aberly on the bottom of the pile.

Caroline pushed away to free the other two ladies of her weight. She was glad to note by their moans and protests of discomfort that each was conscious.

John Coachman's head appeared in the carriage doorway which now tilted to face the sky. His face looked ashen with fear. "Is everyone alright? I can't imagine what happened. Let me help you, Miss."

He reached down and lifted Caroline out of the carriage. Nottington stood ready to help her to the ground. After it had been determined that no one was seriously hurt, John Coachman made a study of the damage.

Lady Aberly brushed her crumpled skirts. "I can't think why you let this coach come in such need of repair as to endanger our travel."

The coachman frowned. "Begging your pardon, my lady, but I don't believe this happened because the carriage was in need of repair. See these lynch pins? Someone replaced the ones that used to be here. These look as though they could never hold a hat in place."

Caroline gasped. "You mean, you believe this accident was deliberately arranged?" She could feel Lavenia's hand shaking as she grasped her arm. "Who would have done such a thing?"

"That's what I'm wondering, my lady," said the

coachman. He turned to Nottington. "Who has been in the stable?"

"Just myself and the two grooms."

The coachman frowned. "Both new, are they not?"

Nottington nodded.

"A bit suspicious," said Lady Aberly. "But why would grooms wish us harm?"

Caroline studied the broken carriage. "One of the grooms was hired by Lord Humphrey." The possible significance gave her a bone-rattling chill.

Lady Aberly shook her head. "I still can't believe he would stoop so low as to harm us."

She turned to Nottington. "If you believe someone has deliberately caused this mischief, you must send them packing."

"Yes, my lady."

"This will take awhile to fix, I presume?" Lady Aberly asked.

The coachman nodded. "I am afraid so, my lady. I had best arrange for your transportation home. Nottington can ride back for the smaller carriage. Though it is too old to be comfortable to travel to Bath, it should get you home in safety."

Lady Aberly nodded. "I do not feel up to further travel today. We will plan our trip when you finish these repairs."

The ladies settled in the shade of a hornbeam while Nottington headed toward the estate.

"I shall take to my bed after this frightful scare," Lady Aberly declared as she administered her fan to her flushed face.

Lavenia cast Caroline a worried glance. "Do you really think Lord Humphrey might be plotting to harm us?"

Caroline shook her head and felt the loose pins that had held her hair in place give way. She ran a smoothing hand to find the loose curls and re-pin them. "I do not know if he wishes us any real harm, but I believe he may have set us up for several uncomfortable mishaps as his way of warning."

Lavenia shuddered. "Such a horrible thought. I tremble to think of what he might plan next."

Lady Aberly broke into the conversation. "I do believe we are getting ahead of the facts. We do not have any proof that Lord Humphrey had any hand in this."

Lavenia brushed a leaf from her skirt. "This is true. But what if he did? What shall we do?"

"We shall marry you off. Then, if Caroline has no desire to marry the Viscount, we shall see that she is safely settled wherever she chooses to go, perhaps back to her family in India or some other relative here."

Caroline felt the blood drain from her face. Her future seemed suddenly bleak. If she did not marry Lord Humphrey, where would she go? She had no relatives, either here or in India. Unable to admit her deceit, she would be trapped. And when Lord Humphrey discovered she did not stand to inherit the estate, would he find a way to dispose of her?

The sound of a coach rattling toward them told Caroline rescue was forthcoming. It rounded the corner and Caroline was surprised to see Geoffrey accompanying Nottington on horseback.

The old ostler stopped the coach and said, "I am sorry

to be so long, but as this coach is so old, I thought as to how I should not rattle it too hard."

Geoffrey dismounted and offered the ladies a hand into the carriage. His eyes slid over Caroline in a particularly concerned appraisal. She blushed under his gaze, her hand instinctively reaching to straighten her bonnet. Why she should care what this groom thought of her appearance still caused her dismay.

The old carriage had been in disuse for many years. The musty smell so overwhelmed the ladies that they were obliged to hold perfumed handkerchiefs to their noses to abide the journey.

Though Lady Aberly rested her head against the corner squabs, her rigid bearing told Caroline she was just as worried about the incident as the younger women.

They arrived at the manor and were helped from the carriage.

"I must say, it is a relief to be home, though I am disappointed to have had our trip spoiled," Lavenia said.

Lady Aberly shook her head. "Indeed. It was been quite an unsatisfactory morning. Perhaps we shall all feel better after a spot of tea and a rest."

She turned to Nottington. "If you fix the carriage today, we shall try again on the morrow."

"Yes, my lady."

Edward swept open the door to announce that their tea was awaiting them in the parlor. Lady Aberly and Lavenia hastened to draw comfort as Caroline followed behind. Before Caroline could step into the marbled foyer, Geoffrey touched her sleeve, displaying a most improper conduct for a groom. "I must speak with you. Meet me on the path to the stable after tea. I will watch for you."

Appalled by his boldness, Caroline intended to rebuke him. The grave expression in his eyes changed her mind. No convention of society could have prevented her effort to hear what he intended to say.

She nodded and turned away quickly, relieved to see that Lady Aberly and Lavenia had already entered the house.

Sparse conversation accompanied the tea and, soon, the ladies drifted apart to seek rest. Caroline lingered in the parlor until she felt sure her companions had retired to their rooms. Heart in her throat, she slipped out the French doors into the rose garden and followed a path that connected with the wooded path to the stable.

She stopped among the roses, taking time to admire them in case someone should see her wandering about. She did not wish it to appear that she was keeping an appointment, but rather enjoying a stroll. If she were glimpsed in clandestine conversation with the groom, she would have no end of explaining to do. And Caroline had no ready explanation.

She slipped into the cover of the trees and paused to master her unsteady breathing. She gasped as someone touched her arm, then turned quickly to see Geoffrey standing behind her, silent as a wraith. He put his finger to his lips and motioned her to step into the forest.

Caroline's heart skipped a beat with the understanding that she had come, unattended, with no one who knew her whereabouts. If Geoffrey was involved in Lord Humphrey's plot, she would have no one to turn to for help.

He drew her into the trees, his warm hand clasped firmly around her arm. Caroline shivered, wondering what had possessed her to trust him. And now, it was too late to turn back.

He released her and, with difficulty, ignored the creamy paleness of her face and soft parting of her lips. He concentrated on the wide, worried eyes that stared into his own.

"Mr. Nottington told me the carriage occurrence was not an accident. I don't mean to frighten you, but there is someone who wishes to inherit the estate. He will stop at nothing to get it."

Caroline assessed him and found only concern in his eyes. "La, but I know that already. It is Lord Humphrey. Did he hire you as well as the other new groom? If so, I am not at all sure I should trust you."

"You may rest assured, my lady, that I have no more interest in aiding Lord Humphrey than you do."

Caroline felt an overwhelming longing to share the details of Lord Humphrey's overtures. Perhaps Geoffrey could help her. Or, perhaps, he was not telling the truth and was merely employed to win her confidence and share what she told him with Lord Humphrey. Was her longing for a knight-errant overcoming her good judgement?

She would proceed with caution. "Lord Humphrey told me life would become uncomfortable if I did not agree to marry him."

Geoffrey's eyes darkened. "He doubtless thought the carriage incident would frighten you into agreement."

"It will not."

"Of course not. We both know he has nothing to gain by such a marriage."

Caroline caught her breath, wondering if he had somehow learned her secret. She turned away. "I am sure I have no idea what you mean."

"Then Lady Eleanor was less than candid with you. If her death wish was for you to inherit her estate, she neglected to have the necessary changes recorded in her will. I have it on reliable source that neither you nor Lady Aberly and her daughter have gained inheritance of Castlegate Manor."

Caroline whirled to face him. "I believe Lady Aberly has lived there for some time. I assumed that she was the rightful heiress to the estate."

"And this is what I wish Lord Humphrey to continue to believe. In truth, the heir is a gentleman from abroad, a great-nephew, I believe."

"How do you know this?"

"I shall not reveal my source, my lady. Let us say I was told in confidence when I was engaged to look into the matter."

"And your master from abroad is hiding behind the skirts of three women so he will not be in danger?"

Geoffrey looked away, the hard muscles in his jaw becomming tight. "The best way to draw Lord Humphrey into a trap is to let him continue in error. I will personally endeavor to see that no harm comes to anyone."

"So, I am to understand you have been hired by this gentleman to depose Lord Humphrey?"

"Have you a better plan, my lady? Perhaps you would prefer to marry him."

Caroline shivered. Geoffrey did not fail to note the effect of his words.

"I do not wish to marry Lord Humphrey."

"Then I have not misjudged your character, my lady. But be wary. I should not be able to abide myself should any misfortune befall you."

Caroline smiled, peering to see his handsome features shaded by the shadows of the trees. "It relieves my fears only to know that you shall be espying the possible misdeeds of the Viscount."

Geoffrey looked into her upturned face and knew if he did not escape, he would pull her to him and claim her lips with a kiss. Such a grave social error would shock her to the core and, no doubt, erase the trust he saw shining in her dark eyes.

She thought of him as a groom, hired by a nobleman to secure his estate from the clutches of the iniquitous Lord Humphrey. He must be careful to sustain that impression. Until he completed the task before him, he must put all amorous thoughts from his mind. He must remember the necessity for this beautiful young lady to remain a lure for the trap he would lay. Yet the longer he knew her, the more difficult it became to believe the risk worth the possible gain.

He studied her face, his thoughts in turmoil. "You had better return, my lady, before anyone suspects ill of your absence." His uneasy emotions made his voice curt.

He turned from her and paced to the stables. Caroline watched the retreat of his broad shoulders, struggling with the confusion in her heart. She had seen the concern in his eyes when he had promised to look out for her. Did his promise rise from a sense of duty or a deeper sentiment?

She picked up her skirts and hurried to the house. She had come here to marry a member of the ton, not a simple groom, no matter how powerful his employer might be. She would carry out her plan. And she would ignore any attempt by her traitorous heart to bewitch her into changing her mind.

Chapter Six

The carriage was repaired and the trip into Bath commenced the following morning. This time Geoffrey accompanied John Coachman to act as footman and protector of the ladies. His formal behavior chilled Caroline after their intimate talk in the woods. She chastised herself for wishing it otherwise.

The conversation of gowns and guest lists lacked the giddy abandon of the day before. Though they had been assured that the carriage had been personally inspected by John Coachman prior to the trip, the occupants struggled with the memory of the frightening misadventure of the preceding day.

Spirits lightened as they rolled across Pulteney Bridge. Safely into town, a sense of security enveloped them. Lady Aberly chatted in light-hearted abandon about the various shops they would visit and the tearoom at which they were to meet Lady Ruyter.

Madame Marian's sign for her establishment came

into view. John Coachman drew the carriage to a stop. Caroline's hands trembled as she disembarked in front of the famous modiste.

Her fears were soon put to ease as the stylish proprietress graciously greeted Lady Aberly and the two young women. "With three such elegant figures, I shall find my creations the talk of the town," she proclaimed, including Caroline in her assertion.

The ladies accepted lemonade and settled into gilt chairs in the elegant workroom with walls of flowered satin silk.

"I trust you have been well?" asked Madame Marian.

Lady Aberly launched into an account of the unfortunate carriage mishap, a story which she now seemed to enjoy retelling. She provided such embellishment and detail that Caroline soon quite despaired of ever getting on with the reason for the visit.

However, after the polite coze, the modiste proved more than efficient. As her assistants brought out various fabrics from the storerooms, Madame Marian lent her advice on the way the dresses might be made up. They examined fashion plates until Caroline thought she should never be able to make up her mind.

Lady Aberly proved more than willing to assist and enjoyed adding her opinion to that of Madame Marian in advising the younger women of the best choice of color, style, and material.

At last, the new ball gowns were chosen and measurements given to the assistants who were to have them ready in ample time. Caroline had nearly collected her nerve to request assistance with riding attire, when Lavenia saved her the necessity.

"Why, Caroline, we have nearly forgotten about your riding habit. You would look so lovely in royal blue velvet, don't you agree, Mother?"

Lady Aberly looked blank for a moment. "I did not know you enjoyed the sport, Caroline."

"I do, my lady. But I fear, in my packing, I neglected to include my attire." Her conscience pricked at the half-truth. She had packed her own wardrobe. Never, in her life, however, had she possessed riding attire.

Madame Marian commenced to produce rich velvets of such quality that Caroline could not choose between the various shades. At last, she settled on a deep blue that brought out the creamy color of her skin.

They left Madame Marian's shop and stepped into the bright sunshine of late morning. A look at Geoffrey, waiting with the coachman, told Caroline why she had taken more trouble with her riding habit than the choice of a gown for the ball. She flushed with embarrassment and told herself she had no interest in impressing the handsome groom.

So why did her heart tremble at his touch as he helped her into the carriage? She must collect her common sense and rid herself of this spell that had been cast over her. She forced her thoughts to the sensible plans she had made for the future. The ball was less than two weeks away. If she could manage without a terrible faux pas, she might meet the man that Lady Eleanor had envisioned for her. She would settle comfortably on a country estate and forget both the danger of Lord Humphrey and Geoffrey's dangerous intrigue.

They took luncheon in a popular tearoom, then journeyed on to the milliner for a bonnet to match the deep velvet of Caroline's new riding habit. When Caroline had found just the thing, a top hat with a lovely gauze veil, she returned to the coach and ventured a covert glance at Geoffrey. The boldness with which he returned the look flustered her and she hurried into the coach.

After a late afternoon stop for Sally Lunn Buns, they were again on their way, clattering out of the city and bound for the estate that Caroline had come to think of as home.

Caroline found herself dozing as the steady pace of the horses lulled her. Her drowsiness was interrupted by the sound of a loud crack. It was immediately followed by a wild careening of the coach as the horses took their heads.

She peered out to see Geoffrey urging Victory alongside the runaway coach. Moments later, a riderless Victory told her Geoffrey had mounted the coach and calmed the frightened horses. As they drew to a halt, she wondered what had happened to John Coachman.

She sprang from the coach, followed more sedately by a pale-faced Lavenia while Lady Aberly remained inside.

"What has happened? Was that a shot I heard?" Caroline asked.

Geoffrey spared her a brief look. "Yes. It caught your coachman in the arm. Nothing too serious, I am glad to report, though it could have been a good deal worse."

While Lavenia hurried to impart news of the injury to

Lady Aberly, Caroline watched Geoffery attend the coachman, marveling at his competence as he helped the man out of his coat and cut away the damaged sleeve. When the wound had been bound with John Coachman's clean cravat, Geoffrey tied Victory to the coach and assisted Caroline back to the carriage.

"We should be on our way before our lingering presence allows us to become the target of another attempt."

Caroline cogitated upon the fact that this was the second time they had been a target. She felt certain now that the shot fired during their first riding expedition had been directed at them.

Once inside, the ladies began to speculate. "Do you still believe Lord Humphrey is behind the mischief that is befalling us?" Lavenia asked Caroline.

"Perhaps not directly. However, I do believe he has had a hand in our misfortunes."

"I wonder who fired the shot." Lavenia still looked pale with worry.

"Someone who knew we had gone to Bath and would be returning along this road," Caroline answered.

Lady Aberly fidgeted with her handkerchief. "Again, you young ladies are making too much of the Viscount's careless words. Our assailant was undoubtedly a highwayman."

Caroline contained her inner thoughts regarding what she thought was an errant opinion. Nonetheless, she remained convinced their assailant was someone who was aware of their whereabouts, someone from the estate.

When they arrived at the estate, the ladies retired to their rooms with the assurance that Geoffrey would attend to the coachman. A long rest and time to think did not change Caroline's opinion as to who lay behind the unnerving deeds. She had believed Lord Humphrey meant only to frighten her, without the intent of harming anyone. With the attack on their coachman, she wondered to what length he might go to assure her compliance.

Unable to sleep, she finally arose and retired to the parlor to find Geoffrey speaking to Lady Aberly. "I have put a poultice on the arm and expect that it shall heal nicely. While he is in recovery, I shall undertake to assist you, my lady, on any errands which need attending."

At Caroline's unobtrusive appearance, Geoffrey found his concentration sorely tested. He longed to stay to tea and chat with her, to see her blush becomingly under his admiring gaze. Yet he knew this was impossible. Considering his position as a groom, it was surely his imagination which had caused him to believe that she had sought his company.

"It is good of you to bring me this report. Geoffrey, is it?" asked Lady Aberly.

"Yes, my lady."

"I do not believe we shall be traveling again before the ball."

She dismissed Geoffrey and Caroline felt the curious racing of her pulse begin to slow.

Edwards brought a pot of tea and a tray of biscuits and tiny sweet cakes. He poured the tea with quiet efficiency, the trace of a worried frown showing on his usually inscrutable features.

Lavenia joined them for tea, still looking pale.

"I do not believe you have recovered from the shock. I must confess I do not believe my own poor heart could stand another such adventure," said Lady Aberly.

Lavenia managed a wan smile. "To think I used to believe our country life dull and I longed to live in the city. I feared our Caroline would languish from boredom after the excitement of London. Of course this was not the excitement which one would enjoy."

"I assure you I have been quite enjoying my stay in spite of these difficulties, which in no way reflect upon your hospitality," Caroline assured her.

Lavenia smiled. "I shall be satisfied to turn our attention back to the ball. When our dresses arrive all our preparations shall be in place."

The dresses arrived only three days later, to the delight of Lady Aberly, who found Caroline sitting in the rose garden with a book she had chosen on the day after Lord Humphrey's visit to the library.

"My dear, you must come see the dresses. They have just come by courier from Madame Marian and she has quite outdone herself."

Caroline followed Lady Aberly upstairs to the sitting room where Lavenia looked a treat in a pale turquoise silk. She held out Caroline's creation of rose silk. "You must try it on. I know you will be pleased."

Caroline took the dress to her room, barely able to stand still while Maggie slipped the soft fabric over her head and attended to the tiny pearl buttons down the back. An overlay of pearl and lace trimmed the bodice and front of the skirt.

Caroline stood in front of the mirror and sighed at the

sight of herself in a new gown, one created especially for her and not altered from those of Lady Eleanor. She twirled and watched the graceful line of the skirt. If not for her apprehensions about her ability to carry off her role, she would be thoroughly looking forward to the ball.

She joined Lavenia and Lady Aberly, now dressed in her pale green sarcenet gown, in the sitting room and had to agree that Madame Marian was indeed masterful in her knowledge of color and design.

Lavenia gushed, "I shall not be able to wait another day to wear this delightful creation. Mother, you and Caroline look so beautiful I shall have to see that Mr. Ruyter does not behold you at the ball."

Lady Aberly blushed. "The excitement has gone to your head. Mr. Ruyter has eyes only for you. Do you not agree, Caroline?"

"I have seen the way he looks at you, Lavenia," Caroline agreed.

Lavenia blushed in turn. "You are too kind."

The ladies returned to their rooms to remove the dresses. As Maggie carefully packed the gown away, Caroline's eyes fell on the box resting on her bed. She removed the wrapping and admired the deep blue velvet of her riding habit. She caressed the soft fabric and wondered if it would elicit an admiring look. She caught her lip as she hung the dress in the wardrobe, realizing whose admiring look she wished to attract.

Dismissing the ridiculous thought, she determined to go for a ride tomorrow. She would seek Geoffrey and ask his advice as to the safety of an outing. After what happened with John Coachman, she did not wish to put either an abigail or Geoffrey in danger.

Two days of steady rain delayed Caroline's outdoor plans. She drifted about the house, helping with ball preparations when possible and spending the remainder of her time in the library.

When, three days later, the sun at last appeared, Caroline donned her new blue habit and slipped off to the stable. The ground smelled of damp earth and leaves. She drew a deep breath and thought again of how much she loved the sights and scents of the country.

She renewed her determination to marry a country squire, for to return to London after becoming used to her life at Castlegate Manor would be a bitter disappointment.

Victory nickered, looking up from his hay as she neared the outside pen. She walked over to pat his nose, only to move away quickly as he nibbled at her delicate jacket.

Laughter behind her sent a flush to her cheeks. She spun around to see the amused light in Geoffrey's shamrock-green eyes. His laughter touched her pride.

"I fail to see what is so amusing."

He assumed a more serious expression. "I have often thought Victory would have been better born a goat. In a playful mood, he has torn some of my best jackets and a pair of fine trousers. And it would be a most opprobrious shame to have any harm come to such a delightful riding habit, if you will pardon my saying so, my lady."

The admiring light in his eyes cast away any offense Caroline had harbored at his previous laughter. Her heart told her this was the reward she had sought when she had envisioned herself clad in the deep blue velvet.

"I have come for a ride if you feel it would be safe. I do not wish to put anyone in danger. However, I cannot believe Lord Humphrey, if he is behind this, has someone always at the ready to take a shot."

Geoffrey nodded, his expression solemn. Caroline noted the cleft in his smooth forehead that formed when he was deep in thought. She tucked her gloved hands into her skirt to still their wayward desire to caress the thoughtful crease from his brow.

Geoffrey glanced toward the stable and the voices drifting from inside. "I think it will be safe to ride. We can talk when we are away from the stable."

He saddled the two horses, then lifted Caroline into the saddle, reluctant to remove his hands from her waist when she was safely settled. Her sweet lavender scent seemed to accompany him as he mounted the spirited Victory.

Caroline glanced at him as they walked the horses toward the hilly grassland. "How is John Coachman?"

"He is recovering. The servants are caring from him in his attic quarters. The wound was not deep. Since there is no sign of infection, I do not believe he will be incapacitated for long."

"I am pleased to hear it. It disheartens me to think that I must be the cause of his suffering."

"You could not have known, my lady, that your presence would put John Coachman in danger. I believe I may know the identity of the assailant."

Caroline brought her horse up short. "I should be most interested in hearing what you have learned."

"As you know, the new stable hand, Benson, was hired by Lord Humphrey. When I questioned him regarding his activity at the time of the assault, he could give me no satisfactory answer and, indeed, seemed most impatient with my questions."

Caroline glanced uneasily in the direction of the trees.

"You need not worry. We can trust Nottington to keep him at the stable. He will find ample chores within his sight to keep the man busy."

"Are you sure Nottington can be trusted?"

"Quite sure, my lady."

"And you think Benson had opportunity to shoot at us and also tamper with the carriage?"

"Ample opportunity, my lady. I was with you when the first shot was fired. So you know that I was not the gunman."

"And the carriage?"

"Four of us work in the stable. Any of us could have had the opportunity to disable the carriage. John Coachman and Nottington were riding atop. I do not think they would have taken the chance of their own injury, nor have they anything to gain from frightening you. I was with you when John Coachman was shot. Again, I could not have been the gunman. That leaves only Benson, who had the opportunity to both shoot and tamper with the carriage."

Caroline watched the play of expression on his handsome features. His words made perfect sense. She wished she had thought of the groom as a possible suspect in contributing to Lord Humphrey's foul scheme.

"What shall we do? We have no evidence," she said.

"I shall endeavor to watch him closely and shadow him wherever he goes. Perhaps I shall catch him in meeting with Lord Humphrey."

"If you could overhear that would be much the better."

He smiled. "You would make a fine investigator, my lady."

She met his approving gaze. "I think not. I would most likely be caught in the act of spying and meet a dreadful end."

"I cannot think of how anyone could wish so beautiful a lady a dreadful end."

She felt her cheeks grow warm. "You speak boldly for a stable hand."

His warm laughter broke forth like a bubbling brook. Caroline quite enjoyed the sound.

"I've been told that I am bold. I like to think of myself as honest and outspoken," he said.

They rode to the outskirts of the Stewart property, where they could look upon the adjoining estate and a small cottage nestled down in a glen.

"I do not miss the bustle and confusion of London when I look upon such a peaceful scene," Caroline said.

Geoffrey studied her, a smile playing upon his lips. "I should think a sophisticated woman such as yourself would miss the trappings of the city."

Caroline shook her head. "I love the country. I should be glad never to leave it."

"Were you brought up in London?"

"No. In India."

Had she been looking at Geoffrey instead of the cottage, she would have seen the look of interest that lit his eyes at her carelessly tossed answer.

"We should go back. I have been gone far too long as it is," Caroline said.

They cantered across the meadow, then walked the horses down the path to the stable.

Geoffrey helped her dismount, a curious expression still lodged in his eyes.

"In what part of India did you reside?"

Caroline felt the discomfort her lies always brought. She glanced up to see that he awaited her answer. Irritation gripped her that she should feel obliged to fabricate an answer.

"Along the coast," she answered vaguely, with a wave that dismissed the subject.

His eyebrows rose. "Were you from the military settlement in Bombay?"

"Yes. That was it."

She turned away too soon to see the surprise that lit his eyes. She knew only that the intimate ride had been a mistake. She must remember her position. The ball and the hope of meeting a marriageable country squire must provide an escape before her wayward emotions led her astray.

Chapter Seven

Caroline sat in front of the mirror as Maggie carefully styled her hair into a becoming upsweep that cascaded down her back in chestnut brown curls. Clad in her new ball dress, she felt like a prized doll being displayed. Her inner discomposure, however, belied the calm exterior which she would endeavor to maintain.

The ball was only a few hours away. And with the ball came her debut into society, a debut that might be fraught with numerous social mistakes. And before the ball, she must manage an intimate dinner with close friends of the family. Anxiety swept over her with the knowledge that Lady Aberly had insisted that Lord Humphrey be invited along with Lady Ruyter and Henry, and the Baron and Baroness Caroline had met at the concert.

When Lavenia had protested the Viscount's invitation, Lady Aberly had been adamant. "We have no proof that he is behind our misfortune. And, since he is family, it would be most indiscreet to withhold the invitation."

Caroline and Lavenia let a look of disquietude pass between them before accepting Lady Aberly's decision. Caroline knew etiquette would demand that she speak to the Viscount. However, she hoped to keep their association as brief as possible.

The hostesses had not gathered long in the drawing room before the guests began to arrive. Lavenia was immediately swept up with Henry while Lady Aberly conversed with Lady Ruyter and the Baron and Baroness, leaving Caroline in the unhappy position of being companion to Lord Humphrey.

He offered his arm to escort her to dine.

Caroline accepted as graciously as possible. He strolled behind the others, allowing time to speak to her privately.

"My dear Miss Stewart, you are looking charming this evening. I believe that dress enhances your consummate beauty."

"Thank you, my lord. I am pleased you approve."

"I approve most wholeheartedly. Have you given our previous conversation additional consideration?"

"Yes, my lord. I will not be intimidated into marriage. And, in this, I think not only of myself, but of you as well. If you were to marry me, rest assured you would be sorely disappointed in the possessions which I would bring."

He glanced down at her and smiled a chilling smile that did not reach his eyes. "I care not for your possessions, my lady. I care only that you are a Stewart. That is all that counts. Lady Eleanor may disown me, but she cannot stop me from marrying back into the family. I will attain what should rightfully be mine. And I suggest that you cooperate."

They reached the table. Caroline did not wish to shock their genteel guests with a cutting reply to the Viscount. Therefore, she could only smile, while seething inside as her mind cast about for a way to end his brazen blackmail. To resist meant sure danger. And yet, even if she were a Stewart instead of an impostor, Caroline knew she would rather die than surrender to his plan.

Though the kitchen staff had prepared a feast fit for royalty, Caroline found her appetite very slight. She forced smiles and polite replies to the Baron who, being almost deaf, spoke so loudly that she feared she would be nearly deaf, too, by the time the meal ended.

The arrival of the first guests for the ball spared Caroline further need to pretend interest in the Baron's conversation. Her attempt to avoid escort by Lord Humphrey failed and she found herself, again, privileged to his intimate overtures.

"I should like the first three dances, my lady, if you would permit me to sign your card."

Caroline shook her head. "It would be improper, my lord, for me to give you three dances in a row since you have made no declaration in form, nor should you, for I would not accept. I shall dance with you as propriety permits."

Extricating herself from the Viscount, she joined Lady Aberly and Lavenia in greeting the guests. Her fragile composure flagged as she struggled to remember the list of names that Lavenia had carefully taught her along with the particular information which went with each guest. She tried to remember the men of political importance, along with whether they were Whig or Tory, the particular matrons of social influence, the fortune hunters, and the men of good family.

With the introductions complete, Henry led Lavenia out to the floor to open the dancing. Lady Aberly and Lady Ruyter sat together watching the couple with obvious pleasure. "He plans a declaration in form this evening," Lady Ruyter confided.

Lady Aberly clapped her plump hands, her eyes following the dancers. "Ah, this is a delightful occasion. I am fond of your Henry and so pleased that he wishes to wed my Lavenia. I cannot wait to see them settled happily together."

She refrained from mentioning her greater relief to see Lavenia rescued from the attentions of Lord Humphrey. She hoped the accusations waged against him proved untrue. She had become fond of Caroline and did not wish to see her married to a man of ill character. However, if someone had to marry the Viscount, she could not help the relief that if should be Caroline and not Lavenia. The thought of settling in the same house with the man set her near to vapors.

She saw the Viscount approach the obscure edge of the dance floor where Caroline appeared to be hiding, no doubt, from the very attentions he sought to impart. His face clouded darkly as Mr. Blois claimed Caroline's attention just before the Viscount arrived. Lady Aberly smiled as Caroline accepted a dance with Mr. Blois and disappeared among the swirling figures already on the floor.

Caroline, though relieved to be spared the company of Lord Humphrey, suffered the dreadful pangs of humiliation as she mis-stepped, causing Mr. Blois to steady her in his arms. Though he gave no indication of objecting to the need to deliver her back onto her feet, Caroline blushed furiously, fearing that she would repeat her mistake.

At the end of the dance, she saw Lord Humphrey bearing down upon them. Caroline favored Mr. Blois with a look of supplication. "I am feeling rather fatigued. I think it is the warmth. May we not sit out this dance and sip punch?"

His face lit with pleasure. "To be sure, Miss Stewart. I should be honored to keep you company with refreshment."

Lord Humphrey appeared at her elbow. "Is your card free for the next dance, my lady?"

Caroline cast a pleasant smile at Mr. Blois. "I am sorry, my lord. Mr. Blois has promised me a glass of punch and his company while I seek a brief respite. Perhaps another dance."

Lord Humphrey bowed courteously, though his dark eyes flashed with displeasure. "I shall await your return to the dance floor with great anticipation."

Caroline's conscience pricked with the understanding that she was leading Mr. Blois to expect her favor. The captivated expression upon his too-angular face left no doubt as to his pleasure at her suggestion to spend this extra time in her company.

To his dismay, he soon found them surrounded by a coterie of young men. Caroline tried to remember which of the admirers were landed gentry and within her plans to captivate. She offered the best imitation of the demure smile she had practiced in front of her looking glass as she chatted, in turn, with each suitor.

She found none of them of particular interest. Her disappointment mounted as she reminded herself that love was not the objective which she ultimately sought. After another poorly executed waltz with a young squire with more land than observable wit and intelligence, she found herself once more confronted by the Viscount.

"I should like the pleasure of this dance."

Caroline paled at the announcement of the impending minuet. The timing, the complicated steps, and the parting and uniting were far beyond her ability to copy what she had observed on the occasions she had served at Lady Eleanor's parties.

"I am fatigued. I shall take a break in the ladies' refreshing room and return shortly. Perhaps then, I shall feel my vigor renewed."

Suspicion glittered in his eyes. "I did not know you were a woman of such delicate constitution, my lady. The accounts I have heard of your riding expeditions would suggest otherwise."

Caroline lowered her voice, not wishing to quarrel. "One should be careful of one's source, my lord. There are those who would tell you anything you wish to hear if they are well-paid for the service."

"Power has a way of commanding loyalty, my dear Miss Stewart. Do not forget that. And I intend to have power. Take your rest, but do not forget that I will not be put off. I am not one to be toyed with."

He left her to her escape with those words of parting. Caroline watched him a moment, his tall figure cutting a path around the perimeter of the dance floor. She felt chilled in spite of the warmth of the room.

Geoffrey stood concealed in the shadows of the rose garden and watched the proceedings of the ball through the open French doors. He suppressed a laugh to see Lady Aberly presiding over the affair with the aplomb appropriate to the lady of the estate. His dealings with her had led him to conclude that she was a simple, harmless woman who liked her life of ease. He begrudged her nothing.

He glimpsed Lavenia swirling gracefully across the floor and understood why her mother believed her mastery of deportment should procure her a proper place in society. Her serene expression and flawless performance were a credit to her education.

Soon she would marry Mr. Ruyter and be out of reach of Lord Humphrey. Her feelings for Mr. Ruyter preoccupied her, though she had proved astute enough in her suspicion regarding the Viscount. Still, Geoffrey grimaced, thinking how little the ladies truly understood the intrigue which threatened the household.

The true object of his search appeared amidst the waltzing figures, looking uncomfortable in the Viscount's arms. Geoffrey's hands clenched unconsciously into fists. Frustration filled him. He was forced to stand outside and watch the sly wretch, Humphrey, dance in a house where the true master dared not safely reside, nor even attend a ball.

He longed to break through the happy dancers and pull Caroline from the arms that held her with possessive confidence. Yet his very position to defend her depended on his keeping his current position. A discharge from his work at the stable would make it more difficult to stay privileged to Caroline's accounts of Lord Humphrey's visits, as well as keeping an eye on Benson.

So, he held his position just beyond the soft glow of light that spilled out from the ballroom. He watched Caroline and knew intuitively that it was more than her displeasure with the Viscount that marred her evening. She danced as stiffly as Lavenia was graceful, depending on her partner to right her occasional mis-step.

She glanced around the room, appearing as desperate for escape as a beautiful butterfly caught in a net. Her distress surprised him. Daughters of the British officers in India were carefully schooled in all the fine arts.

He had not been surprised that she was not a proficient rider. Many young ladies grew up without developing this skill. Yet, her lessons in dance and deportment would never have been overlooked unless, perhaps, Caroline's parents had neglected her education.

He frowned, puzzling over his thoughts as Caroline withdrew suddenly, leaving Lord Humphrey.

She fled as though chased by demons. Her feet took her through the darkened library, out the door and into the rose garden. Her initial relief faded as she wondered what excuse she might make for the extended absence she desired.

She heard the music trickling out from the ballroom.

"Not another minuet!" she moaned. "I cannot dance."

A shadow moved beside her and Caroline gasped. She stifled a scream as she recognized Geoffrey.

"You are in distress, my lady?"

Caroline shook her head, struggling to quiet the pounding of her heart.

"You startled me. That is all."

He stepped closer. Caroline lost all progress she had made to calm herself.

"You said you cannot dance. I am a servant, here to serve you. With practice, and with your natural grace, you should have no difficulty learning."

Before she could protest, Geoffrey swept her firmly into his arms.

"We will begin with a waltz."

"We must not," she sputtered. "Can you imagine what would happen should we be seen?"

She struggled briefly, yet found herself held securely in place as he pulled her forward. "It is dark and everyone is at the ball. We will not be seen."

His masterful leading and her previous practice helped Caroline become comfortable with the flowing steps. He held her close. She could smell the scent of costmary on his clothing.

She knew she must extricate herself from his arms and the danger of discovery they presented. The matrons of influence and young men of property would not be agreeable to the report that she had slipped off to dance with a groom.

Yet enfolded in his arms, the ball seemed far away, existing in a different place than the world she shared with Geoffrey. He released her when the music ended.

Caroline appreciated the cover of darkness to hide the disappointment she knew showed on her face.

"Unless I am mistaken, there will be another minuet next. Here, I will show you the steps."

When the music started, Caroline followed his directions and found that she had made passable progress. Her confidence grew. If she were careful, she would be able to perform the dance without committing a ghastly mistake.

"You are an exceptional dance teacher. What other talents do you have besides that of a groom?" Caroline smiled her appreciation.

"Any number, my lady. Time does not permit me to expand on my mysterious past. We cannot hope to have but one more dance together before your absence may become of concern."

"I shall not forget your kindness in taking pity on my difficulty."

Geoffrey bowed to her courtesy. "Forgive me, my lady, but I am fascinated by your time in India. I understand most young ladies are sent to England for a proper education and training in the arts. How did you escape the rigors of a dance master?"

"My family felt the education provided by the natural beauty of India was quite sufficient."

Geoffrey raised an eyebrow. "They must have been most exceptional people. Has your family been there long?"

Caroline thought back to the bit of family history Lady Eleanor had imparted for Caroline's introduction to Lady Aberly.

"My grandfather is Lady Eleanor's youngest brother. He came to India years ago as an officer."

Had she not been distracted by the complication of the upcoming step, she would have noted the crease of perturbation that formed on his brow.

"Before returning to England I served under Lord Nelson in the battle of Cadiz. Perhaps I know an officer in your family," Geoffrey stated.

"Perhaps. My father is an officer, like his father before him."

Caroline was proud of her ability to recall this detail of Stewart history. Still, the familiar discomfort returned at this need of deception. Luckily, it was only a stable hand with whom she conversed.

He stepped forward in time to the music. "And your father's name?"

Caroline caught her lip between her teeth. Perhaps he knew the officer whose daughter she was impersonating. It would be best to avoid any mention of names.

"I do not wish to discuss my personal history any longer."

"Yes, my lady. Perhaps you would tell me how you liked that lovely dish the Hindu servants cooked of tender beef? Frangipani, I believe it was called."

Caroline felt relief with this question. A matter of personal taste would surely not present the danger that discussing matters of family history presented.

"I found it quite to my liking," she replied with a smile.

The music ended.

Geoffrey released her abruptly. "Perhaps, my lady,

you had better go inside. I have given you all the instruction which I have to offer."

Caroline nodded. "Very well. I remain in your gratitude."

Geoffrey bowed. "The pleasure was mine."

She looked back, gathering her long skirts. She found her reluctance to depart disconcerting. "I shall come for a ride soon. You have proved an apt tutor of riding as well as of dancing."

"Yes, my lady."

Caroline would have heard the flatness of his tone, had she not been flustered by the memory of his touch and the magic of his arms.

She scolded herself as she hurried through the library, back to the company of young men who did not confuse her senses and disrupt the determination that had sent her here. If she did not guard her heart and keep her behavior above reproach she might be forced to return to London and find herself pleading for a position with the distasteful Adela, daughter-in-law to Lady Eleanor. And she would have only herself to blame. As it was, she had allowed, even desired, a breach of proper distance between her position and a stable hand.

Geoffrey's expression clouded with anger as he watched her depart. He had been a fool. She had bewitched him and stolen his heart. He intended to reclaim it before it was too late. How she had come to be in league with the Viscount, he did not understand.

But he felt sure he had been deceived. He took comfort only in the fact that he had resisted the impulse to tell her the identity of the true heir of Castlegate Manor.

Though he had longed to trust her, his natural caution had held him in check.

Even now, he did not want to believe that she was capable of deception. Yet, he could not ignore the obvious truth.

He would uncover her role in the plot. Then, he would see to her downfall as well as to that of Lord Humphrey.

Chapter Eight

Caroline returned to the ballroom and put on a coquettish smile as she danced and flirted with various admirers. She was aware of Lord Humphrey's peevish presence in her small coterie as she alternately filled her dance card, then took her rest and refreshment. Yet her unruly heart compared each partner to Geoffrey and she found each to be a disappointing substitute.

Near the end of the ball, Lady Ruyter and Lady Aberly had the pleasure of hearing Henry declare his intentions for Lavenia. Lavenia blushed becomingly as she accompanied him on a round of well wishes, followed by toasts to their prosperity and good health.

Lavenia took Caroline's hands. "I hope you will be as happy one day as I am right now."

Her words sent a stab of doubt into Caroline's heart. Would she be happy one day? Or would she settle on one of the young men present in order to escape her plight with Lord Humphrey?

He sidled up to her at Lavenia's departure. She sensed his presence before he spoke.

"It seems the fair Lavenia has made up her mind to wed Mr. Ruyter, a decision I find most unwise since he is only to become a baron of small estate. Her loss shall be your gain."

"I fail to see the connection, my lord," Caroline replied coldly.

"Let us not play games, my lady. I can make things most uncomfortable for you if you persist in this ridiculous defiance."

Fatigue and the strain of dancing fanned Caroline's emotions into furor. "Do what you like. I shall never marry you. And you shall never inherit Castlegate Manor."

"You should not say such things. I have told you I will do whatever it takes to become master of this estate. It would be terrible if something dreadful should happen to the existing heirs, would it not, my dear Miss Stewart? You have it within your power to prevent such a tragedy or to allow it to occur. Think about it, my dear."

The dangerous glitter in his eyes chilled Caroline. He turned away and made his courteous departure to Lady Aberly. Caroline would not dream of ruining this merry occasion by reporting his thinly veiled threat. Yet, she chided herself on the irony of her deceitful masquerade should it prove to place her in mortal danger. But she could not tell Lord Humphrey the truth. If it were known, she would have no chance of escaping a destiny in the poorhouse.

After the guests departed and she had gone upstairs to

slip into her nightgown, she lay awake sipping hot chocolate and pondering her choices. If only she had someone she could trust to give her counsel. Lady Eleanor had known her guilty secret and taken it to her grave. If only the dear lady were still alive, Caroline would never have come here, nor fallen into such a disastrous position.

It would be a burden off her shoulders simply to share her true identity with someone she could trust. Mentally, she listed her choices and summarily dismissed them. The shock would be too much for Lady Aberly and Lavenia. Lady Aberly's social conscience would never allow Caroline to remain under her roof should Caroline turn to her as confidant.

Her thoughts turned to Geoffrey. Had he not been retained to resolve the threat to the true heir's interests? Surely he would have nothing to gain by revealing her secret. Yet if he should reveal her identity to the true heir, in time, it might be made known and become an embarrassment to her future husband. She debated deep into the night before falling into a troubled sleep.

She awoke early to a quiet house. Only the occasional subdued voice of a servant convinced Caroline she was not alone on the large estate. Since the ball had concluded at a tardy hour, Lady Aberly and Lavenia would doubtlessly sleep late into morning.

Caroline gave into her impulse and the memory of Geoffrey's competence and donned her riding habit. She paused briefly in the sitting room for a crumpet and cup of tea before striking out for the stable.

The snap of a branch along the wooded path caused her to jump. She glanced fearfully into the brambles and saw a moor hen scoot away with her chicks on their way to the creek below the path.

She admonished herself for letting her nerves rule her mind. No gunman skulked behind a tree; no one followed her steps waiting to harm her. Lord Humphrey had surely exaggerated his threat in order to frighten her.

She found Geoffrey in the stable currying Victory.

He cast her a glance that seemed appraising, then continued his chore as though dismissing her presence. Caroline found his manner disconcerting.

"Do you intend to ignore me?" she questioned.

"You would wish a ride, my lady?" he asked without looking up.

Caroline bit her lip, feeling suddenly uncertain. She had little to lose. Even if she decided not to confide in him, perhaps the fresh air would clear her mind.

"Yes, please see to making my horse ready."

She found some satisfaction in taking command. No matter what might be on his mind, he was bound to do her bidding, keeping her company whether he desired it or not. This one thing she had learned from her years in service.

She waited impatiently for him to bring the horses. Nottington passed by with a polite nod.

"Nice morning for a ride, Miss," he offered politely.

Caroline returned his smile. "Indeed."

She wondered at the arrogance of Geoffrey's manner. Surely, Nottington did not put up with such insolence. The thought struck her that Geoffrey did not truly work for Nottington. He had been hired by the master of the estate. Perhaps he believed this position raised him above the status of the other servants.

"You need not accompany me if you have pressing duties here. I shall not go far," she said.

Geoffrey shot her an impenetrable look. "It is my *duty*, my lady."

Caroline assumed her most dignified posture as they walked the horses down the trail to the open meadow. A palpable tension stood between them. Caroline began to wish she had not chosen to come for a ride.

She cantered ahead to the crest of a hill which looked down to the valley below. Smoke rose from the cottage chimney and a small child played a carefree game of chase with a goose in the yard. She smiled in spite of her pressing difficulties.

She had been too absorbed in her reverie to see that Geoffrey had dismounted and now reached to lift her from the saddle.

She shot him a questioning look. "Is something wrong with the horse?"

"No, my lady. There is something amiss with you, I believe."

She clutched for the saddle, but was too surprised by his action to manage a retaining grip.

He set her rather unceremoniously onto her feet.

"The horses will enjoy the opportunity to devour this sweet grass while we talk."

Caroline rebelled at the firm set of his jaw. They had enjoyed a tender rapport when they had met in the woods to discuss their mutual distrust of Lord Humphrey. Where had it gone?

"I do not like the way you order me about. Hand me back on my horse. I wish to return," Caroline asserted.

He smiled unwillingly. "But I do not wish to return. Not just yet."

She wheeled away. "Then I shall walk back."

He grasped her arm in a grip that frightened and surprised her. She turned to face him and the steely determination in his eyes.

"You shall not go back until I get some answers. I fear you have lied to me and I must insist on knowing the reason for your deceit."

"My deceit?" Caroline had shared her fears regarding Lord Humphrey. She struggled to understand his accusation.

"I have lived in India. And I must inform you that cows are sacred animals to the Hindu. Such a servant would never prepare your beef. And you were quick to concur that frangipani was quite a delectable dish. It is, in fact, a flower that we had in multitude in our gardens. These are things any British lady who has lived in India would know. Why did you not know these things?"

Caroline longed to run, yet she had nowhere to go. Her worst fear had come to pass and now her hopes for the future lay in ruins. Yet, somehow this dismal thought bothered her less than the look of distrust in Geoffrey's eyes.

"You are right. I have not lived in India. For personal reasons, I wished to present the impression that I had done so."

"And why would that be?"

Caroline turned away.

"I beg you not to press me on this. As I said, it is of a most personal nature."

"But, I am afraid I must insist. You see, I have come to the unpleasant idea that your deceit and that of Lord Humphrey may be entwined. If so, I have already confided more in you than good judgement should have allowed."

Her shock deepened that he would accuse her of being in league with Lord Humphrey.

"I assure you, I have no reason to aid the Viscount and everything to lose should he get his way."

"And why is that?"

Caroline met his eyes, her defiance wavering at the accusation in their green depths. She reminded herself that he was only a groom. Still, it was hard to admit her real position in life and see his respect for her vanish.

She pulled from his grip and turned away, fighting the tears that welled in her eyes. "Lady Eleanor wished me to make a good match and live the life of a lady here in the country."

She caught her lip, too aware of his presence as he waited for her to continue. "She wished to help me by allowing me to assume an identity as her great-niece. She even schooled me in a bit of family history. I was to be from India so that no one would question my background in London."

"So you are not related to Lady Eleanor?"

Caroline shook her head.

He turned her to face him. Caroline shuddered beneath the power of his hands upon her shoulders.

"Who are you?"

"I am a maid, a simple ladies' maid. Lady Eleanor employed my parents. My mother was a favorite of hers and we became very close after Mother's death. Lady Eleanor did not wish for me to stay in service. So, she sent me here."

Caroline could feel her cheeks aflame with embarrassment. She did not meet his eyes, nor attempt to extricate herself from his grip. She stood mutely, feeling as though the life had drained from her body, leaving her as lifeless as a doll.

"You are telling me that Lady Eleanor is behind this deceit?" Geoffrey dropped his hands.

"She knew she was dying. So she sent a letter of introduction before I arrived. It is in the possession of Lady Aberly. If only I could procure it, I could prove my story is true."

Caroline stared in shock as he burst into laughter. Her discomfort turned to outrage. "How dare you laugh at me? I don't care if you believe me or not. You are a horrid man. I wish they had shot you instead of John Coachman."

She stumbled away, tears blinding her eyes.

Geoffrey caught her arms and pulled her into a firm embrace. Caroline struggled, mistaking his effort to comfort her as an attempt to take advantage of her newly revealed demotion in social status.

Imprisoned in his arms, she became aware of his words of comfort. "My poor Caroline. I am sorry for what I have put you through. You are not the only one for whom Lady Eleanor has been a benefactress."

She ceased struggling. "Whatever do you mean?"

"Leave it that I have learned that Lady Eleanor has helped another friend maintain an assumed social status."

Her heart was filled with humiliation. Yet as she looked into his face, she was relieved to see that the animosity had left his eyes, replaced by an amusement that she felt sure was at her expense.

He raised his hand and gently wiped a strand of tear-dampened hair from her cheek. "My dear Caroline, do you really think that I care if you are a servant or from the haut ton? I have met many of both high and low position and have liked or disliked many from each."

He bent toward her and whispered softly. "It is not your position which intrigues me. It is you."

His lips claimed hers in a gentle kiss. Caroline reciprocated with a willingness that should have caused her shame. And yet she could not think of anything other than the fact that he had not shunned her. She did not think she could have borne it had he treated her with scorn.

The spell was broken as Victory nudged his nose upon his master's shoulder. Geoffrey pushed him away. "What is it, boy? Can you not stand for me to spend my affection on anyone but you?"

Caroline could not help smiling at the sublime but demanding creature. "I fear I shall not be able to compete with Victory. His bloodline is, no doubt, above question."

Geoffrey cupped her face in his hands and looked into the chocolate-brown eyes that had mesmerized him since he had first seen them. "My grandfather spoke of Lady Eleanor with the utmost respect. If she felt you were a lady of quality, I shall make no quarrel with her judgement. I have seen for myself that she was correct. Your secret is safe with me. Like Lady Eleanor, I shall go to my grave without revealing your past."

"We never meant any harm." Caroline could not express the relief she felt at his promise of secrecy.

"And you have caused none. I fear, however, that you stumbled into danger when you assumed this identity. Lord Humphrey does not know that you are not a blood relative of Lady Eleanor."

"He does not. And I cannot tell him, for he would not be so kind as you in keeping my secret."

"It is not only kindness that motivates me, Caroline."

Caroline was not completely sure of his meaning. "I hope you would not attempt to blackmail me into a compromising position, for I would not agree."

He cast her a disapproving look. "Your lack of charity wounds me. Can you not credit me with as much integrity as I have extended to you?"

His swift reaction gave Caroline no doubt as to his sincerity.

"I am sorry to have offended you. Please understand that it is hard for me to believe that you do not hold my position against me."

"Does this reassure you?"

He kissed her lightly on the lips.

Caroline found herself longing for the kiss to last forever. She managed, however, to gather the presence of mind to say, "Perhaps there are eyes where we do not see. It would not do either of us good to have a witness to this scene."

He smiled. "You are right. We should go back. You cannot know the relief you have given my mind to find that you have no part in Lord Humphrey's schemes. I could not sleep last night for the worry that my fondness for you was misplaced."

"I assure you there are no other secrets hiding in my past."

He helped her onto her horse, then settled himself upon Victory. The sun seemed to shine brighter, the flowers to smell sweet again now that the distasteful matter of his suspicion had been dislodged. He could now smile at the memory of the poor servant girl thrown suddenly into a ballroom.

He watched her small, erect figure cantering just ahead of him across the meadow and felt a measure of pride grow in his heart. Despite the disadvantages of her background, she had done well. Had it not been for her mistakes regarding India he would not suspect the truth. This servant girl possessed more natural charm and grace than many of the well-bred young women to whom he had been introduced and to whom his parents would like him to wed. He deducted that, to a degree, manners could be taught. But the inner beauty of a girl such as Caroline could neither be taught nor feigned.

They reached the stable. Geoffrey turned to her before leading the horses to be unsaddled and brushed. Caroline longed for more intimacy, yet feared the intensity of her attraction to the self-assured groom. If he were to ask for her hand, would she throw her dreams aside and agree? Caroline knew the temptation was growing beyond her ability to control.

She had prayed for the depth of love she had witnessed between Lavenia and her Henry. Caroline wondered if it did not serve her deceitful intentions right that she should fall in love with a groom. She did not deserve a man of high position. Now it seemed as though she would have to choose between love and comfort.

Her thoughts were thus occupied when she entered through the drawing room. She was surprised to see Mr. Blois perched nervously on the edge of his chair. A cup of tea sat untouched upon the table.

He rose swiftly. "It is wonderful to see you. Edwards told me he did not know where you had gone. I see now that you have gone on a ride."

Caroline attempted to smooth her crumpled skirt. "Yes. I have always believed fresh air to be good for the constitution."

Mr. Blois nodded. "And you are positively blooming. I admire a woman who takes care of her health."

Caroline assessed his nervous demeanor and inwardly groaned at the understanding that he had come to make a declaration in form. While she found him agreeable company, she would no sooner marry him than Edwards or the elderly Nottington.

She deftly avoided his attempt to turn the subject to an amorous nature. When Lavenia entered, apologizing for the intrusion, Caroline was quick to invite her to join them.

"Are you sure I will not be interrupting? I only wanted to ask if you have seen Mother. I cannot think where she might be," Lavenia said.

Caroline frowned. Though Lady Aberly often reposed

late, the morning was well-advanced, even for her to lay abed.

"You have not seen her all morning?" Caroline asked.

Lavenia shook her head. "She is not in her chambers. Edwards has not seen her and she is not in the habit of taking a walk."

They sat for tea. Mr. Blois soon excused himself, seeming disappointed that his mission had been less than successful.

Caroline retired to her room to change from her riding attire. A note lay upon her pillow. Caroline approached it with curiosity, then dismay as she scanned the carefully penned warning regarding Lady Aberly.

Chapter Nine

A slow, spreading horror invaded Caroline as she read the note once again. The warning that the safe return of Lady Aberly depended upon Caroline's own choice made it quite clear that Lady Aberly was not missing of her own volition.

Caroline stood uncertainly, peering into her own pale face which stared back at her from the looking glass. Due to the deception Caroline had waged in coming here, she would feel responsible if Lady Aberly were harmed.

Even though the note was unsigned, she had no doubt that it had originated with Lord Humphrey. His veiled threats and attacks upon property and servants had not served to force her compliance. It did not surprise her to learn that he possessed no compunction about stooping to blackmail.

She clutched the note in her hand as she searched the house for Lavenia. She found her in the downstairs parlor in worried conversation with the Baroness, who had come to call on her mother.

Lavenia turned to face her, a worried frown marring her usually cheerful countenance. "I have been telling the Baroness Tarrington that I cannot imagine what has become of Mother. I am nearly beside myself with worry and do not know where to turn."

Caroline composed herself as much as her pounding heart would allow. She pressed the note into the folds of her skirt and wished desperately that the Baroness had not chosen this morning to extend a visit.

"I am sure there is an explanation," Caroline said, attempting to attract Lavenia's attention with the tone of her voice.

Lavenia, however, appeared too upset to understand. She employed the manners her mother had instilled and offered the Baroness a cup of tea.

Fortunately, the grand old lady did not wish to linger and visit with the young women. If Lady Aberly were not at home, she had another matron with whom she wished to pass the morning.

Caroline waited, eager for the Baroness's departure, as Edwards called a footman to escort the woman to her carriage. She did not think she could have borne an hour spent with tea and cakes and speculation as to what was keeping Lady Aberly.

As soon as Lavenia had finished her farewells, Caroline pulled her into the drawing room. Lavenia's questions froze on her lips as Caroline said, "I have word about your mother. I found this note deposited upon my pillow."

Lavenia read the note with an expression of disbelief. "I do not understand. Surely someone could not come into the house and take Mother from underneath our noses."

"I am afraid that is precisely what has happened."

"But how?" Tears filled Lavenia's eyes.

"That, I do not know. I saw nothing unusual when I went for a ride this morning."

"We must question the servants. Perhaps one of them will have seen something that may help us."

Lavenia instructed Edwards to send in the various staff. At the conclusion of the interviews, they were no closer to solving the mystery of Lady Aberly's disappearance.

Edwards cleared his throat. "If it might be of help, I do know that Lady Aberly received a message this morning. I delivered it to her myself."

Lavenia sat bolt upright. "Why did you not speak of it?"

"I am sorry, Miss. I thought nothing of it at the time. The stable hand, Benson, brought it round."

"What did it say?" Caroline asked.

"I do not know, Miss. Lady Aberly did not make me privy to the contents." He raised his chin as though she had implied that he could forget his place.

"Was there a note for me, also?" Caroline asked.

Edwards looked thoughtful. "Indeed there was. As you were out, I had the upstairs maid place it in your room. I assume you found it without difficulty?"

"I did."

Edwards studied the young ladies and, for a moment,

seemed to lose his carefully cultivated bearing. "If there is anything amiss, I should be happy to do all I can to be of assistance."

Lavenia nodded. "Thank you. I may as well tell you that Mother has been abducted. If you see anything unusual or hear anything among the servants that may help us, I would be obliged if you would make it known to me."

Edwards's shocked expression left no doubt that he had been unaware of the foul plot. "My word, Miss. This is ghastly. I shall report any news that may be of help."

"Thank you, Edwards." Lavenia seemed, once again, close to tears.

"Perhaps your mother left the note in her room. It may help us to learn what it said," Caroline suggested.

"Of course."

They found the room as Lady Aberly had left it after she had dressed for the morning. The room still smelled of her cologne and a book lay open on her desk as though she had decided on a break from her reading.

A quick glance around revealed a carelessly dropped note sitting on her writing desk. Caroline read over Lavenia's shoulder and learned that it appeared that the gardener had requested Lady Aberly's presence in the garden for a decision as to which rose bushes she preferred for more plantings.

"The gardener said he had not seen Mother this morning." Lavenia's tone sounded doubtful.

"I'm sure he did not. Did you not hear that Benson had delivered the note? It is possible that he lured her to the garden under false pretenses, then abducted her while no one was aware."

"This is dreadful," Lavenia moaned.

"We must find out if Benson has left his employment at the stable."

They hurried along the path. Caroline had an eagerness to see Geoffrey that transcended their current crisis. Whatever Lord Humphrey's twisted plans to force her into marriage, she knew that Geoffrey cared for her. He would not let her fall into the clutches of the distasteful Viscount.

Nottington was working outdoors, tossing straw into the pens when they arrived.

"Where is Geoffrey?" Caroline inquired.

"Lord . . . Ah . . . Geoffrey is in the stable, Miss. He had a horse what required his attention."

"Thank you."

Geoffrey appeared at Nottington's summons. Nottington returned discreetly to his work.

"We have received the most frightful news," Caroline said.

She handed him the note. "I found this on my pillow. Edwards tells us that Lady Aberly received a note also. Lavenia and I found it in her room."

Geoffrey's frown deepened as he read the neatly penned lines. "She was abducted this morning?"

"She was in her chambers when Edwards delivered the note summoning her to the garden. She thought the gardener wanted to discuss her roses." Lavenia choked back a sob.

Caroline patted the girl's shoulder. "Geoffrey will know what to do."

"Nottington and I will immediately search for tracks. Unless they continued on foot, we may be able to follow wheel tracks in the road. While we are out, we will ask the locals if they have seen anything."

The confidence in his voice soothed Caroline's fears. Perhaps they would find Lady Aberly before the day was over. It would be frightful to spend a night wondering what had happened to the lady.

"Did Edwards say who brought the note?" Geoffrey asked.

Caroline nodded. "It was Benson."

Geoffrey's expression showed disdain. "And he has disappeared. We have not seen him all morning. At least, that tells us who did the abducting. With your pardon, ladies, I shall saddle Victory and see what can be learned."

Lavenia wiped her frightened eyes. "You will tell us as soon as you learn anything?"

Geoffrey's eyes held sympathy. "I will relate my findings as soon as I return."

"Thank you."

Caroline steered the girl toward the house. "There is nothing more we can do. Geoffrey will do all that he can to find your mother."

Geoffrey watched the retreating figures and felt a deep pain. He wondered if it had been right to hide the identity of the true heir when it had put these innocent women in danger.

He had never planned to care deeply for a woman again. After an broken engagement with an officer's daughter, he had sworn off affairs of the heart. But that was before he had met Caroline, who seemed devoid of the subterfuge that characterized the social set he had known in India. Her sweet temper, her lack of the pouts and carefully worded demands of other females, enthralled him.

Caroline seemed a breath of fresh air to his heart. He did not care about her background as a ladies' maid. If this had made her what she was, he could only be grateful.

As he turned to saddle Victory, he wondered if he would be able to equal the trust Caroline placed in him. He would find Lady Aberly and he would protect Caroline, even at risk to his own life. To do less, and betray Caroline's trust, would bring pain worse than death.

Lavenia, nearly prostrate with heartache, had retired to her room. Caroline, for her part, found it nearly impossible to sit quietly and wait for news. She paced the drawing room, growing more restless as the hours ticked away. Where was Geoffrey? Had he any success at finding the trail?

Edwards brought her a light luncheon and cast a sympathetic look as she asked, "Have any of the servants remembered something that might be of use?"

He shook his head slowly. "I am sorry, Miss."

She sighed and resumed her pacing, wishing she might have gone with Geoffrey so that she might know what he had found. To wait and do nothing seemed much harder.

It was after dark when Geoffrey returned. Caroline and Lavenia were sitting in the drawing room, tending to needlework that did not hold their attention.

At Edwards's announcement, they rose so swiftly their work fell to the floor. Yet Geoffrey entered alone, dashing their hopes that Lady Aberly had been found.

Geoffrey disheveled appearance bespoke the long day he had endured. Caroline's hopes sank at the troubled expression on his face.

"I am afraid I have nothing of use to report. We picked up horse tracks leading into the woods, but lost them among the underbrush."

"And no one has seen anything?" Lavenia asked.

"Unfortunately, no. We stopped at cottages and searched the woods until it became too dark to continue. We will, of course, begin afresh in the morning."

"Oh, this is simply unbearable. Whatever can that horrible man have done with Mother?" Lavenia began to sob afresh.

"I suggest you get some sleep. Perhaps there will be better news tomorrow," Geoffrey said.

"I think I shall go up, but I do not believe I shall be able to sleep," Lavenia mourned. "I think I shall have Maggie bring up a cup of hot chocolate."

Caroline placed her soft hand atop Geoffrey's, lingering while Lavenia retired to be attended by her maid.

"Thank you. It is kind of you to be concerned for us," she said.

He studied her, liking the touch of her hand and wishing he could hold it whenever he wished. Honesty told him it was not only kindness which inspired him to search for Lady Aberly. It was guilt.

He looked away without reply. His natural forthrightness nudged him to confess, "I have not been entirely honest with you, Caroline."

Caroline withdrew her hand. The expression on her face punctured his heart. Would she think him a coward?

He took a deep breath and continued. "I have allowed you to believe I was in the employ of the heir to the Castlegate estate. I am, in fact, Geoffrey Stewart, heir to the estate. My grandfather is Lord Stewart of India, of whom you passed yourself off as granddaughter. He had one child, my father. Father died several years ago and Grandfather died last year. Lady Eleanor then named me heir on the stipulation that I return to England and manage her treasured home."

Caroline stared. He read the shock in her eyes as disapproval.

"Do not think I have not suffered for the fact that Lady Aberly is in such straits because I did not make my arrival known. It was a cowardly act, one that I now regret. Yet, it seemed prudent when I first arrived. Nottington informed me that he overheard the Viscount tell Benson that he would murder or marry whoever stood in his way. Since he was not likely to wish my hand in marriage, I presumed murder lay in store for me."

"I am glad you did not let your position be known."

Her voice was so soft, Geoffrey was not sure he had understood her.

She tilted her face to peer at him. "I am glad. I should

have died if I had come to know you only to have you taken away."

His heart settled into a rhythm of relief. She did not hate him. She did not even blame him for the abduction of Lady Aberly.

"Nonetheless, it is my fault that you and Lady Aberly are in danger."

"Your death would have done nothing except put us into the position in which we now struggle. However, in that event, we would not have you to turn to for help."

"I had not thought of it that way." He smiled into her eyes. The temptation of her sweet presence grew overwhelming and he crushed her to him, kissing her fervently before the footsteps of the approaching butler forced them apart.

Edwards paused in the doorway, looking slightly askance. "Is there anything I might get for you, my lady?"

"No thank you, Edwards. You may retire if you like. I am just going up myself."

Edwards nodded. He retreated after casting a last reproving glance at Geoffrey.

"Only Nottington knows your true identity?" Caroline whispered.

"Yes. He served with my father in the military before coming back here to work. He knew me as a boy. That is why I knew I could trust his loyalty."

"As I trust you."

She placed her small hand back atop his own. He picked it up and placed a kiss upon her palm.

"Sleep now, my Caroline. Tomorrow, I shall try again

to locate Lady Aberly. With luck, I may even catch the miscreants as well."

Caroline lay awake long into the night, mixing prayers for Lady Aberly's safety with those of thanksgiving that Geoffrey could still love her in spite of what he knew of her past. She had expected to marry a squire of small estate and keep her guilty secret. It was more than she could have hoped to find a man of fortune who loved her in spite of her lowly position.

The next day yielded no new information in the search for Lady Aberly. Though Henry came and tried to comfort her, Lavenia's reddened eyes and pale cheeks spoke of the despair she suffered.

"You must go to Lord Humphrey. Promise him whatever he wants. I must know what has happened to Mother," Lavenia implored Caroline.

"You mean marry him?"

"He may have a genuine fondness for you. Perhaps it would not be so bad." Lavenia paused in her pleading and surveyed the dismay on Caroline's face. "I am sorry, Caroline. Of course you cannot marry him. The man is a monster. It is just that I am so worried about Mother."

Caroline nodded. "I do understand. And I believe you have come upon a good idea. I shall go to Bath and see Lord Humphrey. Perhaps I may learn something useful."

Lavenia shook her head. "You must not. I am in no state to travel and I would be beside myself with worry that he would not allow you to return."

"I shall take Nottington and Geoffrey with me. And I shall make it very plain that they have orders to see to my safe return."

"Perhaps I should come along," Henry suggested.

Caroline shook her head. "He might not speak as freely with you about."

Lavenia grasped Caroline's hand. "You are brave. I am grateful for your effort on Mother's behalf."

Caroline patted her hand. "I must retire to my chambers and think of a plan. Somehow, I must fool him into revealing the whereabouts of Lady Aberly. I fear it will not be easy, for he is wily and not easily deceived."

Lavenia smiled a wavering smile. "Whatever happens, I shall always be grateful for the effort you make."

When a note from Geoffrey summoned her for a meeting in the rose garden, Caroline had her plan carefully in place.

Moonlight bathed his discouraged visage. "Nothing. Not a sign of her anywhere."

Caroline licked her lips, wondering about his reaction to her plan. "I have given it much thought. As Lord Humphrey is apparently behind this misdeed, it is to him that I feel we must go. If I can make him believe that his plan has failed, he might reveal the location at which she is held."

Geoffrey's forehead puckered in thought. "Do you think he would believe you?"

"I do not see what I have to lose. If you are available to protect me, I do not fear danger. And perhaps I will learn something useful."

She studied his face, eager for his reaction. After what seemed an eternity he said, "I have no better plan. Indeed, I seem to have come upon a dead end. Therefore,

I will agree to this scheme only if you insist upon my being present in the room with you at all times."

"I would have it no other way."

"Then I will tell Nottington to ready the carriage. To-morrow, we will face the fiend together. With any luck, he will tip his hand. Until then, I bid you good-night."

He kissed her gently, then disappeared into the shadows. She shivered as she thought of the horror Lady Aberly must have experienced with an abduction from this very garden. Tomorrow, she would attempt her best play-acting of all.

Chapter Ten

The coach rocked and swayed on its way to Bath. The early morning sun burned through the high clouds, scattering them like a consuming army. Caroline was grateful they would reach their destination before the warmest part of the afternoon. And she was grateful for Geoffrey's comforting presence across from her. Since Nottington had known of Geoffrey's position all along, he showed no surprise when Geoffrey seated himself inside the coach with Caroline.

"Lord Humphrey's attempts to frighten us have set me on edge every time I must travel," Caroline admitted.

"I believe we will be safe as long as Lady Aberly is being held as reward for your compliance in marriage," Geoffrey said.

Caroline shuddered. "I can hardly imagine what horrors she must be suffering, held captive by the likes of those Lord Humphrey would employ."

"With any luck, she will provide the proof to tie the

Viscount in with this evil deed. Then we can send him packing, far away where he will not bother us again."

Caroline smiled. "That does sound good."

They rode in silence until she caught him chuckling to himself.

"And what is so funny, my lord?"

"When you told me you were Grandfather Stewart's granddaughter. Our family in India is quite small. Grandfather had only one child, my father, and he had only one son and daughter. Imagine my surprise upon learning I had a second sister."

Caroline felt her face grow hot. "You make fun at my expense."

He could not resist leaning across the seat to take her hands. She sat stiffly, though not resisting his attentions.

"I do not make fun. I find you delightfully resourceful. You could not have known my identity. I simply find it amusing that you should present your pretense to the one person who would find you out."

His eyes lacked malice. Caroline could not help seeing the humor in spite of her embarrassment.

"I might as well be your sister for the danger I have put myself into."

He kissed her palm. "I am glad that you are not. I like to look upon you and admire your beauty."

She withdrew her hand with proper modesty.

"Tell me about this sister whom I was so foolish as to impersonate."

He sat back in the seat. "She is happily married to an officer and occupies herself with visits to our mother and local gossips."

Caroline frowned. "It sounds rather dull."

"The happily married part?"

"No, the visiting and gossip."

"Perhaps is is because she has no groom to take her riding."

A teasing light danced in his eyes.

"Perhaps," she agreed softly.

She thought back to the intimate conversations they had shared, the fun of sharing the outdoors. "I hope we may still go riding."

"Every day if you like."

"Are you sure you wish to be seen with me? It is possible that someone from London may recognize me someday and disclose my identity. Would that not be an embarrassment to you?"

"Of course not. No one would dare to suggest so humble a background for so fine a lady. And no one would believe them if they did so. They would be left feeling quite the fool."

She lowered her eyes. "You really do not mind? I could not bear to have my former position flung in my face by someone for whom I care deeply."

He raised her chin and gazed lovingly into her eyes. "I will never throw this in your face, nor, with the last breath in my body, would I allow anyone else to do so."

His sincerity touched her to the core and melted her last reservation. "I shall be pleased to have you as my knight-errant if only we have the fairy tale ending that is every little girl's dream."

"Then I shall do all in my power to make it so."

They fell silent as the carriage continued to rock

along. Geoffrey gave into the exhaustion of two long days of searching for Lady Aberly. He nodded into sleep, leaving Caroline content to study his handsome features and wonder how she had missed the sure signs of aristocracy that marked his speech and bearing.

They arrived in Bath late in the morning. Geoffrey suggested taking lunch at one of the fine tearooms before setting out for the Royal Crescent. Caroline felt too nervous about the imminent encounter with Lord Humphrey to do more than pick at her food. Geoffrey ate with the forced discipline of one who has to keep up his strength in battle. Yet, even he could not finish the last of his pork pie.

Caroline noticed the grim set of his jaw as Nottington drove them to the Royal Crescent. They were greeted by a pasty-faced butler who told them that he would inform Lord Humphrey of their arrival.

The Viscount ambled into the room, an assessing look in his eyes that belied his smile. "Why, Miss Stewart, so good of you to come and visit me. And I see you have brought your groom. Did you perhaps think I had a horse in need of tending?"

Caroline did not dignify his question with an answer. "I wish it were a social visit, my lord. However, I have come to inform you of the failure of your latest effort."

Lord Humphrey offered her a stiff-backed chair, then seated himself across the tea table. He raised a brow, the only indication of his interest in the conversation. "My latest effort? I am sure I do not know to what you refer."

"I believe you do, sir. You had Lady Aberly spirited away in hopes to gain the upper hand."

The Viscount dismissed her accusation. "I assure you I know nothing about such a disappearance. If your relative is missing, I can only extend my sympathies. Considering the circumstances of your blatant disregard of my highest intentions toward you, I hardly feel I am obliged to assist you in locating her."

"La, sir. I do not need assistance. It may surprise you to learn that Benson has turned against you. We discovered the location and he has admitted that you were behind the plan. Soon the constable will come for your arrest."

Lord Humphrey narrowed his eyes. His face paled in spite of his obvious struggle to remain composed. "These accusations are ridiculous. I should have you evicted from my presence for even making them. I can certainly assure you that, should Benson fall in with your plot to discredit me, the constable would take my word before that of a man I hired as a groom."

"Perhaps you are right and there is no need to bring charges. After all, Lady Aberly is safe and well. And perhaps Benson acted on his own in hopes of gaining ransom. You know him better than I do. Why do you suppose he chose such a terrible place to hold her?"

Caroline held her breath. If he were to lapse and reveal a clue that would help them, it would be in answer to this question.

Her hopes fell as he sighed in exaggerated patience. "If Benson acted on his own, it is hardly my concern. You have come a long way for nothing. Perhaps you will have some tea with me while your groom sees to the carriage."

He gave Geoffrey a nod of dismissal.

Geoffrey remained at attention a few discreet feet behind Caroline.

"I do not require refreshment and I would rather he remain. I see that we have no case against you, so I plead only that you would satisfy my curiosity. How did Benson choose the location to confine Lady Aberly?"

Lord Humphrey's smile did not reach his eyes. "I am afraid your curiosity will have to remain unsatisfied. If you were to prove more cooperative . . ." He let the words trail off.

"So you admit you have a part in the plot?"

"I admit nothing. I warn that, only in marriage, will you learn my secrets."

"And the innocent will suffer if I do not?"

Lord Humphrey shrugged helplessly. "I wish no one to suffer."

Caroline felt defeated. The interview had not gone as she had hoped. Either he suspected she was lying, or knew the constable would not believe Benson if the Viscount maintained his own innocence. Either way, he had made it plain that he would reveal nothing that might aid them.

Caroline rose. "Our conversation would appear to be over, my lord. So I shall depart."

He grasped her wrist as she turned to leave.

"Not so fast, my lady. Do you not wish to reconsider the advantages of our marriage? My man, Benson, tells me you have been riding alone with your groom. Surely, you know the impropriety of this act. It is not good for the reputation of a lady of fine breeding. If you do not watch yourself, no man of worth will be willing to wed you. I suggest you think about your position. If we wed, you could live in security instead of fear."

Caroline could no longer hold her temper in check. His threat to blackmail her reputation was more than she could bear.

"Unhand me this moment."

Geoffrey stepped forward.

The Viscount released Caroline and reached into his waistcoat. Caroline was horrified to see the glint of a pistol. She feared that he would murder them both.

Yet his hand froze and his eyes hardened. She spun to see Geoffrey already holding a pistol aimed at the Viscount's chest. A spell of dizziness nearly claimed her and made her realize she had been holding her breath.

"Get out of here, both of you," the Viscount growled.

Geoffrey backed out of the door, following Caroline.

The butler showed them out.

Caroline drew a breath of fresh air and tried to force her trembling legs to carry her out to the street, where she was relieved to see Nottington waiting beside the carriage.

When they were settled for the ride back to the estate, Caroline turned to Geoffrey apologetically. "I am afraid I was not clever enough to gain the needed information. I hope I have not made things worse for Lady Aberly."

"You must not blame yourself. The Viscount is a shrewd man."

"Nonetheless, I shall be sorry to report my failure to Lavenia. She has been terribly upset about her mother."

They left the cobbled streets of Bath and turned onto

the country road. Caroline had just rested her head against the corner squabs for a rest when the sky broke forth with torrential rain.

Their progress slowed to a crawl as the wheels splashed into the muddy ruts. Caroline shivered as dampness permeated the carriage. Geoffrey saw her discomfort and removed his jacket, insisting she place it across the shoulders of her light summer frock.

Her grateful smile warmed his heart.

He watched her, entranced by her fragile beauty, as she again rested against the carriage. His heart told him that it was ready to trust again. Here was a woman who would not break it. Whatever she lacked in bloodline was more than compensated by her sweet smile.

The rumble of another carriage passing them on the path roused Caroline from her rest. She pushed aside the curtain to see a man peer at them briefly before closing his curtain to the rain.

Geoffrey frowned. "If I am not mistaken, that was the doctor who was out to care for John Coachman after he was shot."

Caroline felt her pulse quicken with alarm. "They were coming from the direction of Castlegate Manor. The Viscount could not possibly have issued an order to avenge my visit in the time since we departed Bath. Do you suppose someone is ill?"

"Perhaps. I agree that Lord Humphrey has not had time to exact vengeance."

Caroline fidgeted with the lace on her skirt. "Perhaps I should have told the Viscount that he would not benefit by holding Lady Aberly. If he knew that I stood to inherit nothing he might release her."

Geoffrey shook his head. "We have come too far for that. Such a confession would more likely endanger her life."

Caroline caught her lip with her teeth and tried not to shiver with a chill in her spirit that even Geoffrey's coat could not keep out.

They reached the manor just as Edwards was lighting the outside lamps. Geoffrey took her hand as Nottington drew the horses to a halt.

"I shall wait in the rose garden behind the library should you need to see me after supper."

"If I can slip away, I will come," Caroline promised.

The footman helped Caroline out of the coach. Edwards held the manor door open, looking disapprovingly from the pouring rain to Caroline's dampened attire.

"I shall go up and change before supper. Please send Maggie to help me," Caroline instructed.

"Yes, my lady."

In the upstairs hallway, Caroline saw Lavenia disappear into Lady Aberly's doorway. She listened a moment and, hearing no sound of conversation, felt her hope disappear.

Maggie arrived to help Caroline slip out of her damp, mud-splattered dress and into dry clothes. After she had brushed and arranged Caroline's hair for supper, she commented, "I am sorry to have been slow getting to you Miss, but we been ever so busy with the mistress come back."

Caroline wheeled from her seat at the dressing table.

In her haste, she upset a strand of curls Maggie had arranged atop her shoulders.

"Do you refer to Lady Aberly?"

"Yes, my lady. She came walking back this morning. We heard she was stolen away for ransom. I do not know how she escaped, but she must have been ever so brave."

"Yes, Maggie, I am sure you are right."

Caroline rose. "My hair is acceptable. You may return to your duties."

"Yes, my lady."

Caroline could hardly wait to see for herself that Lady Aberly had returned. She prayed the lady would suffer no lasting effects from the ordeal.

She met Lavenia when she stepped into the hallway. Lavenia put a finger to her lips and motioned Caroline back into her bedchamber. She closed the door quietly behind them.

"Have you heard that Mother is back?"

Caroline nodded. "Maggie just told me. How is she? It must have been a dreadful ordeal."

"She is very weak. The doctor was here this afternoon and gave her laudanum to help her rest. He said she must not talk until she gets stronger."

"You do not know how she came to escape?"

Lavenia shook her head. "She was too befuddled when she arrived to be coherent. But the important thing is that she is back. The doctor believes that she will recover completely."

Caroline felt tears well in her eyes. "I am so glad. I dreaded reporting to you that my visit to Lord Humphrey yielded nothing of use. But now your mother has safely returned."

After supper, Caroline accompanied Lavenia for a brief visit to Lady Aberly. The older woman slept with the peaceful look of a child despite the graying hair that spread haphazardly across the pillow.

"She was very restless until the doctor got her settled," Lavenia explained. "She kept mumbling about the man who got shot."

"I wonder who that could have been?"

"It might have been Benson."

They spoke in whispers so they would not disturb Lady Aberly. She was nearly as pale as the sheets and her face thinner than Caroline had remembered.

"Do you suppose she had to shoot him to make her escape?" Lavenia's eyes held a worried look.

"I should guess she did not. And if she did, I am sure it was her only choice."

Lavenia failed to appear comforted. "Might not such a memory torment her? She was so peculiar, not at all herself when she came home."

"I am sure it was only the fatigue and strain. She will be herself when she awakes. You will see."

Caroline left Lavenia sitting with her mother.

She slipped down to find Geoffrey waiting in the garden. The rain had stopped and the sky was partly clear. The moon slipped from behind a cloud, illuminating them in its light.

Before she could speak, he strode forward and took her into his arms. "I could hardly wait to see you again and know that you are safe. This unfortunate business with Lord Humphrey has made me quite wary for your safety."

She smiled up at him, enjoying the comfort of his embrace, and was greeted by a tender kiss.

"We shall be seen if you are not careful," she reprimanded gently.

"Let them see. In time, you will be my wife."

The promise warmed her heart. "I shall hold you to that, and if you find another love, I shall torment you mercilessly."

Her teasing words drew a smile. "Never. I will never love anyone else."

"And neither shall I."

Though she longed to continue their intimate exchange, she felt pressed to proffer the news about Lady Aberly. She extricated herself from his arms and ignored her desire to forget all unpleasantness. Until the unfortunate business with Lord Humphrey came to an end, none of them were safe.

"I must tell you the news of Lady Aberly. She has returned while we were away."

She heard his intake of breath. "Was she harmed?"

"It does not appear so, though I understand she was in quite an agitated state."

She proceeded to tell Geoffrey the few details she had learned regarding the return of Lady Aberly.

"We can only hope, when she is herself again, that she may offer clear testimony of Lord Humphrey's hand in her abduction. The authorities may not believe a groom, but they will listen to a lady of her stature," Geoffrey stated.

Caroline nodded her agreement. "I do hope that is the case. I shall wait eagerly for her recovery so that we may learn the whole story and discover who was shot."

Caroline noticed Edwards lingering in the parlour door, staring into the darkness.

"He must have heard our voices. I must go in," Caroline said.

Geoffrey stole a quick kiss before disappearing into the night. Caroline waited until Edwards was satisfied that no one lurked about, then slipped into the parlor and up to bed.

It was two days before Lady Aberly felt well enough to give an account of her experience. Caroline asked Geoffrey to join them as soon as she heard that Lady Aberly planned to leave the confines of her room and come down for tea. Settled in the sunshine of the downstairs parlor, still looking wan, she began to give an account of her ordeal.

Chapter Eleven

Lady Aberly had been settled comfortably into a stuffed chair for several minutes when Lavenia pleaded, "Now you must tell us what happened, Mother. We have all been waiting until you should feel like talking."

Lady Aberly heaved a great sigh. "I should like to pretend I had never received that note, nor ventured into the garden. The ordeal has given me migrims."

"I know, Mother, but what happened?"

Lady Aberly glanced around the room. Her eyes fell on Geoffrey. "What is he doing here?"

Caroline was not sure she could trust Lady Aberly to keep Geoffrey's true identity a secret.

"He has worked with Benson. I thought he might be of use in helping us predict Lord Humphrey's next move. Do you not now believe that Lord Humphrey is behind our misfortunes, my lady?"

Lady Aberly shook her head. "La. I do not know what to believe."

After a moment of silence and a sip of tea, Lady Aberly continued. "You know that I received a note, supposedly from the gardener, requesting my presence in the garden. Since he knew how much I loved my roses, I was not at all suspicious regarding the request. However, when I got to the garden, this terrible man told me that Morgan was around the hedge, if I would be so kind as to come along."

Lady Aberly paused and dabbed a lace handkerchief at her eyes. "When we were out of sight behind the hedge, he seized me roughly and put his foul hand across my mouth so that I could not cry out. Someone else, a larger man, I think, wrapped a cloth about my eyes and tied my hands behind my back. Then, the two of them hastened me toward a waiting horse."

Lavenia's hand flew to her mouth in horror. "Oh, Mother, how terrible for you."

"It was terrible. We rode for hours, jostling about until I was so stiff I could hardly walk. Finally, we stopped. They held me in a small stone cottage that smelt of grease and dirt. I have not a clue to the location, as I was kept blindfolded the entire time of my captivity."

She shuddered, then continued. "When I was left alone for awhile, I felt my way about the room, but could find no way of escape. The door was bolted from the outside and the windows must have been too high for me to locate without benefit of my sight."

"Had you nothing to eat?" Caroline asked.

"La. They fed me twice a day, if you would call such gruel food. Each time, they warned that if I took off the blindfold and caught sight of them it would be my demise. You cannot imagine the trepidation I was under."

Lady Aberly fanned herself with her lace handkerchief.

"Did you hear their names?" Caroline asked.

"I did. It was on the morning I escaped. I shudder to think of it. They took me out of the house and led me into the woods. One man called the other by the name of Benson. When Benson complained that I had heard his name, the other man told him he was not to worry, as they had been ordered to do away with me."

"No, Mother! How simply ghastly. Thank goodness they did not succeed. How ever did you get away?" Lavenia asked.

"They began to argue. Benson told the other man that he had not planned on murder when he made the bargain. The other man told Benson that he could forget his share of the money if he did not have the stomach for the work. The blindfold had slipped a bit, so as I could see a little. The bigger man shoved Benson. They were in each other's faces and shouting. While they were occupied and not attending to me, I edged away. I pulled off the blindfold and ran into the woods. Then I heard a gunshot. At first, I thought it was directed at me, but as no one seemed to be following, I decided that one of them had shot the other."

She paused, the haunted look in her eyes showing it would be a long time before she would be rid of the memory of her ordeal.

"And you kept on running?" Lavenia asked.

"Yes, until I was so out of breath I had to stop and

rest. I feared at any moment I would be captured. But no one ever came. I wandered the woods, quite lost until I came upon the road. I followed it all the way home."

She closed her eyes and laid back her head. Her pale cheeks gave her a ghostly pallor. Caroline wondered if she had fainted.

Lavenia gently chafed her wrists. "Mother, are you all right?"

Lady Aberly opened her eyes. She patted Lavenia's hand. "I only hope you never have to go through such an ordeal, my precious. I have given great thought to keeping you safe until the wedding."

"How is that, Mother?"

"The three of us—you, myself, and Caroline—shall all journey to London. We shall stay with Lady Adela. I am sure she will have the household running smoothly, though I must say I will miss Lady Eleanor most frightfully. We shall make the final purchases for your trousseau. Would you not like that, my dear?"

Lavenia's eyes lit with delight. "I would love it, Mother. You are so clever. I will miss Henry terribly. But it is only three weeks until the wedding. And it will be nice to be somewhere where we are safe. Do you not agree, Caroline?"

Caroline felt as though her heart had frozen in mid-beat. She shot Geoffrey a frantic glance before she managed to reply, "Perhaps I should see to things here while you are gone. London is so busy and I am still quite enjoying the country life."

"Nonsense. I would not think of leaving you where you might suffer such a trial as I endured. You will be back to the country in time for the wedding," Lady Aberly assured her.

Geoffrey watched the play of emotions that crossed Caroline's fragile features. He longed to scoop her up and rescue her from the well-meant and unintentional trap in which Lady Aberly had placed her. Since such rash action would not be advisable, he set his mind to devising a scheme to deliver her from the awkward situation of leaving Lady Adela's house as a maid and returning as a relative.

Caroline grasped for an excuse. She thought of two pretexts and summarily rejected each in turn. If she pleaded illness, Lady Aberly would refuse to leave her and likely send for the doctor. If she pleaded a pressing engagement in Bath, Lady Aberly would offer to postpone the trip until Caroline was free.

In her panic, no clear plan presented itself. At last, Caroline simply nodded and said, "It is kind of you to include me." She hoped her face did not show the distress lodged in her heart.

"Then it is all settled," Lady Aberly announced, sounding more cheerful.

Pleading fatigue, the lady had her maid escort her back to her chamber, leaving Lavenia and Caroline with Geoffrey.

Lavenia turned to Geoffrey, her eyes wide. "I have never liked the Viscount, but I did not think him capable of ordering Mother's death. Can we not have him arrested?"

Geoffrey shook his head. "We have no proof that he ordered her kidnapping or execution. Lady Aberly gave no account of having seen him while she was held by the other men, nor did she hear them mention his name."

Lavenia sighed. "I suppose you are right. He would deny his complicity and we would look like fools."

"We will not live in his tyranny forever. He will make a mistake. You will see," Caroline said.

"This distress for our daily safety is sure to give all of us migrims. I am glad the three of us will be away in London for awhile," Lavenia replied.

Geoffrey smiled at Caroline, giving assurance that he did not believe she was easily given to migrims. She returned the smile, though Lavenia's reference to London had, again, put her in a stew.

Before departing he offered, "If I think of anything that might be useful in your travel plans, I shall be happy to offer it."

He retired to his room above the stable to think. Though Lavenia had thanked him, he hoped Caroline knew the words were meant for her. He would do nothing else before he thought of a plan to spare her humiliation.

Before the afternoon was out, he knew precisely how Caroline could avoid the doomed trip to London. All he had to do was make a few simple arrangements and get word to her.

Unfortunately, it proved more difficult to deliver a message than he expected. He appeared at the back entrance to tell Edwards that he wished to see Miss Caroline. He was surprised when Edwards told him crisply that he would not allow any more messages to be passed by the grooms unless he heard them first himself.

Though Geoffrey appreciated the effort of the stiff-necked butler to protect his mistress and the two young ladies, it was going to be hard to arrange for a meeting with Caroline. And yet, he must get word to her and end her worry.

He need not have fretted over his failure with Edwards. After tea, when the ladies retired for rest, Caroline slipped from the house to meet Geoffrey at the stable. He hurried to greet her, delighted to have his problem solved. After a quick glance to be sure no one was watching, he took her in his arms.

"Edwards, in his overzealous protection, would not let me see you. I do believe he has acquired a distrust for grooms and the truth of the messages they bring."

Caroline smiled, the worry momentarily fading from her dark eyes. "I cannot say that I blame him. The last groom to bring a message proved quite dishonorable."

"I am not dishonorable, Caroline, though you make it very hard not to embrace you each time I am in your company."

"Would not Lady Aberly truly faint at the liberties I have allowed between our assumed positions? She would be positively scandalized."

Geoffrey laughed. "She would indeed."

Caroline sobered. "But whatever shall I do about this trip to London? I have thought and thought. Yet I cannot find a way to avoid the trip and still not arouse suspicion. I simply cannot show up at Lady Adela's and face the humiliation that would bring."

"And you shall not need to do so."

"You have a plan?"

"I do. I shall pen you a note stating that your return to India is eminently required. I shall state that it is a family emergency." He added humorously, "Edwards may even read the note if he insists."

"But that will not work. Lady Aberly will surely insist on seeing me off on my ship."

"Ah, I have thought of that. I shall pay the porter to smuggle you on and, before the ship departs, he will smuggle you off. We will spend the night in separate rooms of the local inn. You may be assured my intentions are entirely honorable. The next day, you and I will spend a delightful day in Bath while Lady Aberly and Lavenia continue on their way to London."

Caroline's dark eyes filled with hope. "Do you think it would work?"

He brushed a finger along her soft cheek. "Of course it will work."

"How will I explain my presence when they come back to Bath for the wedding? I cannot possibly tell them that I managed to return from India so soon."

"You need only tell them that we discovered the note to be a fraud, an attempt by Lord Humphrey to lure you away so that he might take control of the estate. Tell them that I warned you just in time to leave the ship."

Caroline sighed. "A lie upon a lie. I feel all I am telling these days are lies. However, I guess I have no choice."

"It is not entirely a lie. It is true that the note will request you to return to India and it *will* prove to be a fraud."

She smiled. "You are right and quite clever, I might

add. I could never have thought of such a plan. I do not know how I shall ever repay you."

His eyes glinted mischievously. "I shall think of something once we are married."

She blushed furiously, to his amusement.

"I think, my lord, that we should keep our thoughts upon our immediate problems, not that I am unwilling to entertain plans for marriage."

He nodded, stifling his desire to continue his teasing. She looked so girlish and charming with her lashes lowered above her rosy cheeks. He must remember to incite her to further blushes once they were married.

He forced himself to cast the promising thought from his mind and dwell on the note which she would present to Lady Aberly.

"Since you are agreeable, I shall pen the note this afternoon. Where shall I meet you to put it into your hand?"

"I will walk in the garden after sunset. Perhaps you might find an excuse to meet me then."

He raised her hand and kissed her delicate palm. "I shall be waiting."

Caroline forced herself to withdraw before he should make any further display of his affection. She still worried that word of their pairing would reach Lady Aberly or Lavenia. And it was still too dangerous to reveal Geoffrey's secret.

Lady Aberly, who seemed to have regained her robust health, spent the afternoon in a flurry of packing for London. Lavenia popped in and out of Caroline's room asking for advice and inquiring as to the progress of Caroline's own packing.

In order to keep up the charade, Caroline was forced to go through the motions of choosing clothes and packing valises, though she felt silly knowing they would go no further than the harbor at Bristol.

She looked forward to meeting Geoffrey in the garden and escaping the bustle of activity that only reminded her of her deception.

Lady Aberly kept up a constant stream of talk about London during supper. "We shall shop at the fine shops and add to your trousseau," she told Lavenia.

She turned to Caroline. "And we shall take in a play and perhaps a concert. It really is too bad that Lady Eleanor's failing health prevented you from experiencing London society on your previous visit."

"That would be delightful." Caroline forced herself to feign interest.

At the conclusion of the difficult meal, Caroline was dismayed to hear Lady Aberly say, "I should fancy a walk in my rose garden. Would you dear girls accompany me? I fear it will take me some time to feel comfortable venturing forth alone after my terrible ordeal."

"We should be happy to, should we not, Caroline? It will be a nice break from all our packing."

"Yes. It would be lovely."

Caroline's heart sank. She would have no chance of speaking to Geoffrey privately while flanked by her companions. And he would have no chance to deliver the note.

The garden bore the lovely smell of roses in full

bloom. The height of summer and recent rains had coaxed the fragrant flowers into large profuse blossoms.

Lady Aberly took a halting step down the cobbled garden path, then paled. "It is hard for me to forget how that horrible man maltreated me in my beloved garden."

Lavenia patted her shoulder. "It will be all right, Mother. We will walk with you."

Lady Aberly caught her breath as Geoffrey strode into the garden. Caroline feared the woman would faint. Both she and Lavenia placed steadying hands upon her arms.

"It is alright, Mother. See, it is only Geoffrey," Lavenia coaxed.

Lady Aberly fanned herself with her large ornate fan. "Whatever is he doing here?"

Geoffrey bowed. "I am sorry if I startled you, my lady. I found a letter to the attention of Miss Caroline which appears to have been dropped in the carriage lane. I feared it might be important and wished to deliver it personally into her hand."

Lady Aberly muted her frantic fanning. "I see. I suppose that is acceptable."

Caroline's heart beat quickly as she took the letter. She had hoped to read it before she pretended surprise at the contents. Perhaps this unexpected circumstance of delivery would make her reaction more believable.

Geoffrey made his expected departure and Caroline tore open the missive. She scanned the lines while Lady Aberly and Lavenia waited expectantly.

"Bad news?" Lavenia asked.

"I am afraid so. I am asked by my family to return to

India at the first possible departure. I am afraid I shall not be able to accompany you to London after all."

"Good gracious. I think I had better sit down." Lady Aberly established herself upon a stone bench and resumed her vigorous fanning. "So much has gone amiss, I hardly dare look forward to each new day."

Caroline felt quite guilty at the concern which filled Lavenia's face. "I do hope it is not a dire concern which demands your return, though I am sure it must be so. You have been here such a short time and I did so look forward to a longer visit."

"I must admit I find this most unsettling. I rather expected to make my home in Bath," Caroline admitted truthfully.

"But it is your family and you must go. How shall you book passage?" Lavenia asked.

Caroline gave a proper moment for thought. "I shall send Geoffrey to obtain my ticket from Bristol, then I shall depart on the first ship."

Lady Aberly recovered her wits enough to say as Caroline had expected, "We shall, of course, see you off before we begin our trip to London. I should send an abigail to accompany you on your trip, but with the upcoming wedding, I don't know who I can spare."

"It not necessary to send an abigail. I am sure I shall find a matron aboard to chaperone me as I did on the voyage over. And you need not see me off. I know you are in a hurry to reach London," Caroline protested politely.

"Nontheless, I must make personally sure that you arrived safely at your destination. Lavenia and I can be all packed to continue to London as soon as you board."

"That would be very kind."

They remained in the garden, enjoying the onset of evening. Caroline felt wicked, knowing the two women expected it would be one of their last days together. She wished she could spare them the sadness of a parting that would end as soon as they returned from London.

Yet, as she was forced to play her part, she stayed with them until Lady Aberly declared that her fatigue required her to retire. They walked upstairs together. Lavenia paused at Caroline's bedchamber.

Impulsively, she put her arms around Caroline. "It will not be the same in London without you. You seem almost a sister to me now."

"As do you."

Alone in her room, Caroline went about the task of packing her belongings for a very short trip.

Chapter Twelve

Geoffrey left at sunrise the following morning to purchase passage for Caroline's trip. He returned that evening holding a package that Lady Aberly and Lavenia were to assume held Caroline's passage to India. She was to leave the next afternoon.

"So soon?" Lavenia protested.

"Are you not ready to leave for London?" Caroline asked with some concern.

"Oh, yes. Mother and I can both be ready to leave on the morrow to bid you good-bye. Still, I hoped you would not sail for a few more days."

Caroline shook her head. "The sooner you are in London, the safer you will be from Lord Humphrey. When I am gone, he may turn his efforts toward you."

"That would be frightful. I should die if anything prevented my marrying Henry as planned," Lavenia declared.

"Then we shall have to be very careful that does not happen."

Caroline spent a restless night in a state of nerves, fearful that some detail in the ploy had been overlooked. In the morning, the footman loaded her bags onto the coach. John Coachman, now recovered from his injury, helped them aboard.

As they rolled onto the drive that led from the great estate, Caroline cast a glance from the curtained window of the coach. She caught sight of Geoffrey watching discreetly from the distance of the stable path, and her heart warmed with assurance.

She was not alone in this mad scheme. Geoffrey would follow and make a clandestine arrival in Bristol. He had already arranged for the porter to rescue her from the ship. Then, after an overnight stay in the city, they would hire a coach to take them back to Bath, where Nottington was to meet them and assure them that Lady Aberly and Lavenia had traveled on to London.

She sat back in the plush seat and tried to relax. She had a great deal of traveling to do and it would not do to exhaust herself when she had barely begun.

The weary hours crept by. Caroline's tension mounted when they finally arrived at the bustling port in Bristol.

The footman helped them from the carriage. Caroline found the ship, a tall passenger line already bustling with porters. While the men gathered her traveling bags, she lingered with Lady Aberly and Lavenia.

"I do so hate good-byes. I hope you will come back to us as soon as you can," Lavenia said.

Lady Aberly dabbed at her eyes. "We shall miss you, dearie."

Caroline hugged them each in turn, her conscience pricking her with accusations of dishonesty. If she were really leaving, she would share their same deep regret. The knowledge that it was all a ruse made it difficult to pretend grief.

As she boarded the ship, she paused and pulled a red rose from her reticule to carry in her hand, the signal to the porter of her identity.

Excited groups of chattering passengers trod along the gangplank. Caroline joined them, turning to wave at Lavenia and Lady Aberly as the huge white ship rose above her. Her heart beat madly. If there were any mistake, could she indeed find herself on her way to India? What then? The possibility was too frightening to contemplate.

Members of the crew greeted the passengers as they stepped aboard. Caroline held her rose in prominent view. One young man with black hair and dark eyes waved in recognition. She sighed with relief when he made his way toward her.

In a low voice he confided, "If you will follow me, Miss, I can show you your escape."

Caroline followed him onto the ship and down a narrow flight of stairs. The musty smell of the air made her long to climb back up to the deck.

He paused before a small cabin. "Slip in here, Miss, and change quick into the porter's outfit. Be sure and put your hair under the cap. No one will know you when you slip back down the gangplank."

Caroline stepped into the cramped room and saw the

white shirt and trousers lying across the narrow bed. She shuddered as the porter closed the door and waited for her in the hall. The idea of appearing in public in men's clothes appalled her. Of all the deception she had waged so far, this seemed far the most risky and scandalous. She wondered what Lady Eleanor would have thought of the turn her well-meant plan had taken.

However, as she seemed to have little choice, Caroline slipped out of her gray muslin traveling dress and into the ship whites. She adjusted her cap in front of a small cracked mirror, and, when she felt satisfied that not a strand of long chestnut hair had escaped, she opened the door to find the young man still awaiting her emergence.

"I believe I am ready."

He grinned as he gave her a quick perusal that set her cheeks aflame. "I must say, Miss, I have never seen a more attractive sailor. If you keep your head down, though, I do believe you will pass unnoticed."

"What about my reticule?" she asked, glancing down at her hand baggage that now carried her gray muslin traveling dress.

"Just take it down like you are taking it to a passenger. The gentleman that hired me said you should keep walking until you were told to get in a carriage."

She followed the porter back on deck. The gangplank was nearly devoid of passengers, the ship nearly ready to sail. Lady Aberly and Lavenia peered intently up at the rail, trying to catch a last glimpse of Caroline.

Caroline kept her head down as she disembarked. She walked past the line of well-wishers, so close to Lady Aberly and Lavenia that she would have laughed at the subterfuge had she not been so terrified of being discovered.

A footman stopped her as she wove her way behind the crowd to the waiting carriages. "This way if you please."

Caroline followed him to a curtained hackney. He opened the door, and to her relief, she saw Geoffrey waiting inside. He smiled broadly at the sight of her.

His eyes roved over her trousered form. "This is a sight I never thought to see. You make even the meanest attire look attractive."

Caroline settled as far back in the seat as the carriage would allow. "This was certainly not my preference of what I would choose to wear. When will I have opportunity to change?"

"I have arranged to stop at an inn on the outskirts of Bristol. You may pretend to be my servant and change in my room. I have reserved another chamber for my *sister*, whom I said would be joining me, although I wish she were already my wife."

"I can think of nothing I would like more."

She began to relax as the carriage moved away from the harbor. All had gone as planned. Surely, she was now safe from discovery.

She allowed Geoffrey to hold her hand as they traveled along the busy streets to the outskirts of town where a small inn sat, looking lonely by comparison to the buildings along the crowded streets.

Caroline felt a resurgence of anxiety. Would her attire attract attention? She could not wait to be rid of it and, yet, if she were caught leaving Geoffrey's room after she changed, she would never forget the humiliation. It was all most unsuitable, and unfortunately, most unavoidable.

Her fears were relieved when the owner of the inn, a short balding man of middle age, barely gave them a glance. His attention was absorbed by a serving girl who had dropped and broken a favorite mug. Caroline pitied the girl who was receiving the rough edge of his tongue. At the same time, she was grateful that her own appearance got little notice.

Most of the guests were already in the dining room, leaving the halls empty. She slipped into Geoffrey's upstairs chamber and changed into her dress. Then, leaving the porter's uniform folded upon the bed, she peered into the hall where Geoffrey was quietly waiting.

He greeted her with a smile. "I must say, you look quite back to your usual radiance, and a suitable dinner partner. Shall we go down and procure our meal?"

Caroline met his approving gaze. "That would be most welcome. I must admit, I am famished."

"I must tell you we will be joined by a young lady I have met."

"A young lady?" Caroline froze on the steps, her hand on his arm."

He patted her hand. "Do not frown. I knew you were uncomfortable with the circumstance of being here with me without an abigail. I arranged with the local vicar for his daughter to act as your companion for the evening. She believes that you are my sister and that you are leaving school in Bristol to travel to my estate. I told her we would need her services for one evening only."

"It was kind of you to consider my reputation," Caroline replied.

The young lady who was to be her companion waited just inside the door of the inn. She was only a young girl, barely in her teens.

Geoffrey introduced them.

The girl's name was Ann. She curtsied and made polite reply before following them in to dine. The girl seemed quite uncertain of herself until Caroline asked kindly, "Do you help your father in his duties as vicar?"

"Oh, yes, my lady. My sisters and I take the soups that Mother makes to the sick in our parish."

Caroline smiled. "You and your sisters must be a true blessing to your parents."

Ann blushed and visibly relaxed.

They concluded a pleasant supper, then a walk in the back gardens of the inn. Geoffrey was careful to keep the conversation away from any subjects that would arouse Ann's curiosity as she followed behind them.

Caroline felt pleasantly tired when Geoffrey escorted them back to the bedchambers. After a chaste good-night at the door, Ann and Caroline entered their chambers while Geoffrey departed for his own room.

"Will you be quite comfortable here, away from home?" Caroline asked the young girl.

"Yes, my lady. It was ever so kind of your brother to let me take on such a pleasant job with a lady like yourself."

Caroline smiled at the compliment, pleased that the girl did not question her posture as a lady.

"You must be tired, Ann. I know I am quite fatigued,

myself. You may take the small bedroom in the back and retire as soon as you desire."

The girl seemed relieved to find her evening was nearly at an end and that she would earn money badly needed by her family for this small service of keeping company with a lady.

"Then I will bid you good-night, Miss. Please call if there is anything I may do for you," Ann said.

Ann tucked herself away in the back room and blew out her candle. Caroline lay in the dark, savoring the opportunity to drop her guard.

She slept deeply, awakening to Ann's gentle touch on her shoulder. "Your brother says it is time to get ready, Miss."

Caroline could not, for a moment, remember how she came to be in the strange room. She stared at Ann until her memory of the day before flooded back.

"Thank you, Ann. I see that you are already dressed. You may go ahead to meet your father if he is here. I shall be out in a moment."

"Yes, my lady." Ann paused at the door and turned back to Caroline. "I hope you enjoy your new home in Bath. It was a pleasure to meet you, my lady."

"It was a pleasure to meet you too, Ann."

After a light meal of tea and biscuits, Caroline and Geoffrey began the journey to Bath.

"I shall be so glad to get back to the estate. I have missed it," Caroline said.

"A traveling life is not for you?" Geoffrey asked.

"I should be content to settle at Castlegate Manor and never set foot from the estate."

"You really could be content there, could you not? What a blessing to have a wife who is pleased with her lot in life," Geoffrey mused.

She watched him and wondered if he were thinking of a personal experience. Tact would not allow her to question him about such a matter, so she waited for him to continue.

"Many of the girls I knew in India wanted a great deal more than a country home to keep them content," he explained.

"Perhaps I do not expect more because what you offer is far above what I ever expected to attain."

IIe leaned forward. "Do you know how hard you makc it not to seize you in my arms and cover you with kisses, my sweet Caroline?"

She drew back and tried to look dismayed. "You must not say such things when we are alone, my lord."

He laughed heartily. "Would you prefer that I say them when we are in the presence of others?"

She joined his laughter. "Of course not."

They spent the pleasant drive to Bath chatting over plans for their future. As they neared the city, they both grew quiet. Caroline knew Geoffrey shared her ominous feeling regarding Lord Humphrey when he said, "I have asked Nottington to make discreet inquiry with Lord Humphrey's servants as to the recent whereabouts of their master. Perhaps he will find something of use."

"I do wish we could find some way to end this dangerous affair. I shall never feel safe as long as he is determined to become master of the manor. And if he discovers your identity, you shall not be safe, either."

Geoffrey took her hand, enjoying the softness of her glove. "But we shall be safe. I shall find a way to be rid of the threat that the Viscount presents."

"I hope so. I should not want to marry you only to worry that you might be murdered at any moment."

"You shall not lose me. This is one battle the Viscount will not win."

The carriage left them off at the Circus.

They lunched at a small tearoom, then walked about while Geoffrey gave her a tour of this part of the town.

"Nottington is meeting us back at the Circus late in the afternoon. Until then, our time is all our own," Geoffrey told her.

She had managed to put the Viscount from her mind and was having a marvelous time when they stopped for afternoon tea. The sight of Lady Ruyter with an elderly woman brought her back to her senses.

Caroline whispered, "What shall I do if I am seen with you? How shall I explain?"

"She has never seen me. Simply tell anyone you meet that I am an old friend from India," Geoffrey suggested.

Lady Ruyter greeted them politely.

"Caroline, it is such a pleasure to see you. I assumed that you accompanied Lady Aberly and Lavenia to London."

"I was going to do so, but some unavoidable business detained me in Bath."

"What a pity." Her eyes fell on Geoffrey.

"I would like you to meet an old friend from India, Mr. Geoffrey . . ." Caroline hesitated.

Geoffrey bowed. "Geoffrey Nelson, my lady."

Caroline gave him a quick glance.

She must remember in future introductions that he had borrowed the last name of his favorite military leader, Lord Nelson.

Lady Ruyter nodded. "This is my mother, Lady Amelia. You must join us for tea. I want to hear more about India."

"If you are sure we are not intruding," Caroline replied, wishing she could think of an excuse to decline.

"I insist," returned Lady Ruyter.

They joined Lady Ruyter and her elderly white-haired mother.

It was a relief to have Geoffrey present to regale the ladies with true stories of India and exciting accounts of battles with Lord Nelson.

Caroline was required to do very little talking and the time passed quickly.

After polishing off a pot of tea, Lady Amelia stated, "I have enjoyed our visit very much but my daughter forgets that I covet my afternoon nap. I shall be required to seek our departure."

"It was lovely meeting you," Caroline offered sincerely.

Lady Amelia smiled graciously. "It was lovely meeting you too, my dear, and your charming friend."

After the ladies departed, Caroline and Geoffrey took a slow stroll back toward the Circus. It felt so right to Caroline to be walking beside Geoffrey, her hand tucked in his arm.

She had quite forgotten that Mr. Blois officed near the Circus and that it was time to end work for the day. As they passed his establishment, they came face to face with him as he descended the steps.

"Why, Miss Stewart, what a pleasure," he began.

His smile faded as he took in Geoffrey's presence at her side. Caroline snatched her hand away. Her face grew as warm as though she were a small girl caught stealing a pastry.

"Mr. Blois, how nice to see you," she returned. "I would like you to meet Mr. Nelson, an old friend from India."

Caroline knew she would someday be caught in these lies. She only hoped by then it would not matter.

Mr. Blois bowed, his expression carefully guarded. "How nice to meet you, Mr. Nelson. I hope that you shall have a nice visit in Bath before you return to India."

Geoffrey surveyed the young man and the covert look that he gave Caroline.

"I shall not be returning to India, Mr. Blois. I have decided that a country life is more to my liking and Miss Stewart has encouraged me to stay."

"I see." Mr. Blois bowed again before adding curtly, "Miss Stewart, Mr. Nelson, good-day."

Caroline fought back laughter as the young man trod down the street in a huff. "I think you have discouraged my only suitor, Mr. Stewart."

"If you are waiting for an apology, I can assure you it shall not come."

They sobered as they spotted Nottington waiting for them at the entrance to the Circus.

"Perhaps he has some news." Caroline felt her pulse quicken.

"What did you learn?" Geoffrey inquired of the old ostler.

"Lady Aberly and her daughter left for London early this morning."

"Good. Then it is safe for us to return," Geoffrey stated. "Did you learn anything about Lord Humphrey?"

Nottington nodded. "I did some checking with Lord Humphrey's servants. I found a footman whose lips could be loosed with a shilling. I am afraid, though, that you might not like what I learned. This morning, Lord Humphrey also left for London."

Chapter Thirteen

Lord Humphrey had made it known that he wished his carriage ready early that morning. The servants had gone about their duties with an urgency that bespoke the master's impatience to be off. His destination had been a fact entrusted only to the butler. However, because his servants felt little loyalty, before the carriage left the gate, everyone including the cook and the scullery-boy knew his itinerary.

The butler swabbed his forehead as the carriage drove out of sight. He guessed the other servants shared his relief to be rid of the irritable Viscount, who had been in a rare old mood, snapping at everyone for the last week. The servants knew that something had gone wrong and chalked it up to gambling losses.

The butler sighed as he turned back to his duties. He feared that if the Master continued to combine his lavish lifestyle with his customary bad luck, his butler would soon be looking for another employer.

The Viscount sat stiffly in the carriage, unaware of the glorious scarlet sunrise that ushered in the new day. A morning fog, gray and drizzly, would have better suited his mood. He smoldered at the botch made of his plans by Benson and his associate.

He had regretted the order to dispatch Lady Aberly, not because of any personal solicitude, but because his plans had been frustrated to such a infuriating degree by Caroline that he was driven to risk murder. He could not have known the two men he had entrusted with the task would murder each other instead and let the intended victim escape.

Now, he must chance allowing his interest in the estate to be made known in London. He would call upon Lady Aberly's solicitor and have the particulars of the will explained to him. Perhaps he would learn of some other way he could depose Lady Aberly, the stubbornly surviving heiress.

He arrived in London on the second day of his travel. It was late and the solicitor's office was closed. The Viscount settled upon an inn not far from the office. He had a belated supper, then headed for the local pub where he incurred more gambling debt and a dizzy head from his potables.

The next morning, he awoke in a surly state to demand his footman bring round the carriage while he choked down coffee and a light breakfast. He intended to see the solicitor as soon as possible.

He arrived to find that the office was not yet busy. An apprentice showed him into the plush office of the departed Lady Eleanor's trusted solicitor, Mr. Grable.

Mr. Grable greeted him with a bow. "Good-day, Lord Humphrey. I hope that I may be of service to you."

He was a short fleshy man of advanced years. His quiet, deferring manner bespoke his position of service to the gentry of London. The Viscount pegged him as a man of refined tastes. Perhaps they would do business together.

"I think you shall be able to help me. I know my great-aunt had the greatest respect for your judgment."

Mr. Grable smiled, showing even white teeth. "She was one of my favorites, a very great lady. I have missed her immensely."

Lord Humphrey nodded. "I fear she may have been in a declining mental state in the last months of her life. She had told me she intended to amend her will." The lie rolled easily off his tongue.

Mr. Grable frowned. "She mentioned nothing to me."

"I believe her health prevented her from making the changes that she desired. Lady Aberly is not suitably caring for the estate and I fear it will fall into disrepair."

"Lady Aberly?"

"Lady Eleanor's niece, I believe."

"Lady Aberly did not inherit Castlegate Manor."

The Viscount sat forward in surprise. "You will have to excuse me. I was not able to attend the reading of her will. However, I was informed by Lady Aberly that she had become heiress."

"I am afraid she was mistaken. I can show you quite plainly that it is not true." Mr. Grable called for his clerk.

"Fetch Lady Eleanor's will. I shall read it to this gentleman."

Lord Humphrey sat in silent astonishment as Mr. Grable read the contents of the will. He had no interest in the London estate which was rightfully left to a son and his wife. The country estate named a grand-nephew, Geoffrey Stewart of India, as heir.

He sat in silence as the reading was concluded.

"And Mr. Stewart? Has he come forward to claim his estate?"

Mr. Grable shook his head. "He has not. It is quite a mystery, as he had written saying he planned to come over from India. He has surely had time to arrive by now."

"Did you ever hear Lady Eleanor make mention of her grand-niece from India, a Miss Caroline Stewart?"

"I cannot say that I have."

"I see."

Suspicion formed in the Viscount's mind. Had Caroline accompanied her brother from India, then kept his identity hidden? If so, someone must have overheard the plans the Viscount had made to dispose of anyone who stood in his way.

Caroline had called the groom Geoffrey. He had arrived suddenly at the stable. Suspicion turned to understanding. The young man Benson had reported Caroline going on unchaperoned rides with someone who was, no doubt, her brother. That explained it.

Lord Humphrey rose from the over-stuffed chair. "You have been a great help in clearing up my understanding of the will. If this gentleman from London does not appear, I will return to stake my claim upon the estate, as I am also a grand-nephew."

Mr. Grable nodded. "Indeed, it would seem likely that it would be Lady Eleanor's next intent."

"Then we shall likely meet again."

Lord Humphrey strode from the office, letting his visage change from studied mildness to rage that he had been blind to the truth. He had wasted time, time that had been costing him a nice profit to pay off his debts.

"Drive to the West End. I wish to visit the home of the departed, Lady Eleanor." He slung the words in caustic command to the waiting coachman.

They arrived in London's fashionable West End and found the home now occupied by Lady Eleanor's son and daughter-in-law. Lord Humphrey had been there on occasional visits to London with his parents before their deaths.

Lady Eleanor's disapproval of his father had extended to include his entire family, something which the Viscount had not forgiven her. Now he would have the final revenge. He would thwart her wishes and have her beloved estate for himself. But first, he had to understand how Caroline fit into the plan.

He presented his calling card with the butler.

"The master is not home at present. I shall see if Lady Adela will see you."

He returned to escort the Viscount to the parlor. "The lady will see you momentarily. Please make yourself comfortable. I shall have tea delivered while you wait."

Lord Humphrey fought his impatience as he watched a maid deliver his pot of tea. On impulse, he asked, "Do you remember a Miss Caroline who lived here just before Lady Eleanor's death?"

"A Miss Caroline, sir? The only Caroline I remember was a lady's maid to Lady Eleanor," she answered timidly.

"Lady's maid?"

"Yes, sir. This Caroline served here ever since she was a small girl."

"I see."

Lord Humphrey fell silent. He was so deep in thought, he nearly forgot to rise when Lady Adela made her appearance.

"I am sorry to have kept you waiting, my lord."

Lady Adela gushed with charm. She wore a pink gown that did not become her middle-aged frame, but make her look foolishly girlish.

Lord Humphrey bowed. "I hoped that you might supply me with information, my lady. I wish to locate a young woman who lived here before Lady Eleanor died. Her name is Caroline."

Lady Adela frowned. "The only Caroline I remember was a maid, a special favorite of Mother. She disappeared without bothering to give leave just after dear Mother's death."

"I see. And you have no idea where she has gone?"

"I do not. The ungrateful wretch simply disappeared. It would not surprise me if she had gotten herself in some kind of trouble. If I may be so bold as to ask, is that why you seek her, my lord?"

"Indeed, she has stolen something from me and I wish to get it back."

"She must be punished, my lord."

"I quite agree. I see you are a woman of sound thinking. I have left a card with my address. I shall be returning to Bath. Would you be so kind as to contact me if this young woman should return here?"

"I would indeed. Now will you not sit and finish your tea? I have two guests also from Bath staying with me at present, Lady Aberly and her daughter. It is too bad they are out at present."

"It is regrettable indeed." Lord Humphrey covered his surprise at the close call.

For his trouble to learn Caroline's identity, Lord Humphrey was forced to endure the tedious company of Lady Adela. However, it seemed a small price to pay for the information he had gained.

At long last, Lady Adela flagged in her unceasing prattle and Lord Humphrey was able to make his departure.

"I am in your service, my lady, for your kind hospitality and the information you have given me."

Lady Adela tittered. "I was pleased to be of service. Do call again when you are in London. Perhaps my Herbert will be home and you may stay for supper."

"I should like that."

The Viscount tipped his hat, then hastened to his carriage.

He had new plans to make, ones that would not be pleasant for those who had deceived him.

The news that the Viscount had left for London had put Caroline in a rare state of nerves. She turned to Geoffrey in a panic.

"We must warn Lady Aberly and Lavenia. He must surely mean them harm."

"Indeed, you are right. But I shall go alone on Victory. It will be faster than taking the carriage."

Caroline nodded her agreement, though she would have liked to accompany him.

She watched as Geoffrey set out at once from Castlegate Manor. Her heart constricted as both magnificent horse and rider disappeared behind the line of trees. She did not want to think of what danger Geoffrey might find himself in if he interfered in the plans of the unscrupulous Viscount.

The next two days passed slowly. Caroline passed the hours reading in the library and walking in the rose garden. She dared not let herself think of the danger facing those she loved.

On the third morning alone with the servants, Caroline found her walk interrupted by the unwelcome presence of Lord Humphrey. A hulking brute of a man accompanied him.

Caroline nearly stumbled against them as she rounded the corner of a hedge.

"How pleasant to see you, Miss Stewart, is it? Where are your kinswomen, my lady?" His voice was thick with sarcasm.

Caroline felt her blood run cold. "You know perfectly well they are in London, my lord. And if you have done them any harm, you will answer to the constable."

"You are in no position to make threats, my dear girl."

Caroline backed toward the hedge. The large man who accompanied the Viscount circled behind her. Caroline was not sure of their intent, but if the cold expression in the Viscount's black eyes gave any indication, it boded ill for her.

She turned to push past the large man, hoping to surprise him and gain entrance to the house before he might stop her. But he had anticipated her reaction and caught her roughly, entrapping her with his trunk-like arms.

Before Caroline could call for help, he placed a beefy hand across her mouth, muffling her voice to a sound no louder than that of a crying kitten.

"Bring her to the horses," the Viscount commanded.

Caroline found herself dragged from the garden and handed as roughly as a bag of turnips onto a horse behind the Viscount. The other man mounted and they turned the horses toward the woods.

"You had better hold tight," advised the Viscount.

Caroline found she was obliged to accept his advice. They cut through a path in the woods that was barely wide enough for the horses. Branches scraped across her arms as she hunched unwillingly against the Viscount's broad back.

She longed to protest, to reason with him, but the rapid pace of the horses and her effort to remain seated kept her mute.

By the time they paused to let the horses drink at a small stream, Caroline felt her arms would no longer hold her onto the horse. She fell exhausted upon the stream bank. "You are making a terrible mistake. I am not who you think I am. Forcing me to marry you will not get you what you want," she said.

She shrank under his dark gaze.

"I know precisely who you are. I made a visit to Lady

Adela. It seems she knows of no Lady Caroline. However, she remembers quite well a servant girl who fits your description."

"It is true. But you have nothing to gain by holding me."

"That is where you are wrong, my dear girl. Like your Geoffrey—and do not look so shocked, I know all about Geoffrey—my feelings for you do not depend upon your position. Once I have gained Castlegate Manor, I intend to have you, too. And you shall agree."

"I shall not," Caroline argued quickly.

"I think you shall. You see, I have the power to make sure you do not find employment. Indeed, Lady Adela already believes that I search for you because you are a thief. It would be no difficult matter to have you arrested. You would remain there until you agreed to be released into my custody. And I do not believe you would like the conditions."

Caroline shivered. The horror of such a choice made her feel weak with revulsion. But she would not have to choose. Geoffrey would come for her. He would not let it end like this.

But Geoffrey did not know what had happened. He had gone to London to protect Lady Aberly and Lavenia.

Her mouth went dry. "You were in London. Did you harm Lady Aberly or Lavenia?"

"I did not. You see, I had Lady Eleanor's solicitor read me the will. It seems I was mistaken in believing that Lady Aberly was the heiress. She is no use to me."

"Did you harm Geoffrey?" She could hardly get out the words.

"Not yet, my dear Caroline. But I shall."

They resumed their pace, coming at long last upon a wider path that led to a small stone cottage. Caroline could think of nothing except the Viscount's threatening words.

She longed to escape, to rush back to Geoffrey and warn him that the Viscount had learned his secret. Tears ran down her cheeks as Lord Humphrey shoved her roughly into the musty cottage.

The large man produced bread and cheese and stale water from a pouch. Caroline refused refreshment, then thought better of it. She needed to keep her strength should the opportunity for escape present itself.

The Viscount turned to her when they finished the simple meal. "Make yourself comfortable, Caroline. You shall be here for some time. My accomplice and I must make plans, so I will bid you good-night. You shall be locked in and Edgar shall stand guard outside, should I depart. Even so, I think it best that I tie your hands, so you will not entertain any silly ideas of escape."

He looped a rope snugly around her wrists before leaving her alone in the house. She paced the room, unable to make herself consider lying down on the dingy blanket that covered the narrow bed.

She glanced up at the high windows liberally laced with cobwebs and realized, from Lady Aberly's description, this must have been the same house where she was imprisoned. The Viscount had told her, during their meal, that Lady Aberly's guards had killed each other. Caroline feared she would not be as lucky. She would have to find another way of escape.

Her hopes faded as the shadows grew long. She had pried at the two windows until her fingers ached and her bound wrists grew sore. At last, she climbed down from the rickety chair and gave up her efforts. The windows were wedged tightly shut, the door bolted. Her prison held her secure.

She laid her head upon the table and wept.

She did not remember falling asleep. Yet sunlight filtered through the dirty windows when she sat up with a start as the oaken door creaked open. The Viscount appeared carrying more bread for her breakfast.

"I am sorry I cannot offer you a finer meal. But, as you can see, circumstances do not permit me to bring along my cook. Perhaps this hardship will make you all the more grateful when you are installed in luxury as my wife."

Caroline stared at him, feeling he must surely be mad. If so, reasoning would gain her nothing.

"What do you plan to do to Geoffrey?" she asked.

The Viscount rubbed his chin as though deep in thought. "Let me see, I have sent Edgar this very morning to place a note with Nottington to give to Geoffrey when he returns from London. The note proposes a trade. He will sign away the estate for me, and in return, regain the woman he loves."

Caroline shrank from him as he attempted to cup her chin.

"Yes, my dear Caroline, you are tempting bait. He will come for you and he will come alone as I have required. It is regrettable that he will meet with an accident before he arrives."

With a scornful laugh, he left her alone to regard her unappetizing meal. Caroline pushed it away.

She had wanted, with all her heart, for Geoffrey to come and rescue her. Now she hoped that he did not.

Chapter Fourteen

In London, Geoffrey waited until he saw Lady Aberly and Lavenia leave the house before calling upon Lady Adela. Lady Adela, being a woman unused to frequent attention from gentlemen, made him quite welcome.

"You say you are a friend of Lady Aberly and her daughter? It is a pity that you have just missed them. You are the second gentleman to call upon me in the last few days. The other man inquired about a servant girl who worked here. Quite an unpleasant matter. I do not like to speak of it."

Judging by her loquacious manner, Geoffrey believed she would impart any sort of gossip. He decided to press for information. "Did you catch the gentleman's name? Perhaps he is someone I know."

"Yes. He left a card in case the girl should come back here. She stole from him, you know."

Lady Adela flitted to the lamp table and presented the card.

"Lord Humphrey," she said. "Do you know him? He seemed quite the fine gentleman. He was most polite."

Geoffrey tempered his reply. "We are acquaintances. I shall keep my eyes open for this girl. Did he ask for her name?"

"He did. I told him it was Caroline. I remember her well. She worked for Lady Eleanor for many years."

"Did he say where he was going when he found that Caroline was not here?"

"Yes. Back to Bath, I believe. He thought he might find the girl there."

Geoffrey was gripped by sudden trepidation. If the Viscount had discovered the truth, he might have gone back to seek Geoffrey. Caroline was there, alone and unprotected. What might he do with her?

"Thank you, Lady Adela. You have been most hospitable. I shall have to call upon Lady Aberly when I am next in Bath."

"Will you not say and finish your tea?"

"I am afraid urgent business demands my departure. Perhaps another time I may enjoy your charming company and that of your husband."

The corners of Lady Adela's lips, painted a shade too pink, drooped with disappointment at losing her guest. However, she answered politely, "It was a pleasure, sir. I do hope you will come again."

Geoffrey mounted Victory and turned toward home. He only hoped to arrive and find that his worst fears were unfounded.

* * *

Nottington frowned at the departing lummox who had brought the note. Coming from the likes of him, it could not be good news. Nottington wished to open it. Yet, it stated clearly that it was for his master.

He tucked it away and wished that Geoffrey would hurry and return. The house servants were all a-dither. It seemed Miss Caroline had not appeared for supper, nor come home the next morning. Now, there was gossip that she had run away.

Geoffrey did return late the next evening, having ridden poor Victory nearly to the grave.

"Take care of him, will you, Nottington? I have ridden hard. I must see about Caroline."

"Then you know, sir?"

Geoffrey whirled, a frown creasing his brow. "Know what?"

"That she has not come home. Been missing for over two days."

Geoffrey's fatigue vanished in a rush of fear. "Did anyone see her leave?"

"No. But you got this note today. Came from a bloke I never seen before."

Nottington drew the note from his pocket and handed it to Geoffrey.

Geoffrey scowled as he read the fine script.

"I should have known better. I should not have left her."

"Is it bad news, then?" asked the old ostler.

"She is being held in exchange for my signature disclaiming my rights to the estate. I am to follow this map to a meeting place in the woods."

"You cannot be thinking of going. It could be a trap."

"I have no choice. He will hold Caroline until I come, and I cannot bear to leave her in his clutches one moment longer than I must."

"You must wait the night, have a rest and a meal."

Geoffrey glanced at the cloudy sky, with not even the moon to guide his way. It was as though all was against him.

"Yes. I shall wait the night. I would not have enough light to follow the right path." He sighed in resignation.

Nottington turned his attention to the horse. "You cannot take him out again anyway. I have never seen him so done in."

"We will both take a night's rest and start at daylight."

Geoffrey joined Nottington for a light meal that he did not taste, then tossed restlessly under his covers. It seemed forever until the sun made a weak attempt to light the sky.

He dressed hurriedly and pocketed cold biscuits to serve as his breakfast. He did not know when he would have the chance to have another meal. He vowed it would be after he had returned Caroline safely to the estate.

He was not so foolish as to believe the Viscount would allow him to live once he had signed the papers. With this thought, he kept a sharp lookout as he picked his way through the woods. At a turn in the path, he halted and scanned the foliage.

The sharp smell of damp earth filled his nostrils. A butterfly fluttered away. A rabbit hopped across the trail. The forest was alive with creatures. And, somewhere out among them, he feared one far more dangerous than any of these gentle inhabitants.

He rode on slowly.

He might have missed the man poised for ambush had the glint of a gun not flickered from the foliage. He drew his weapon and shot into the brush. He heard a grunt of pain and knew the bullet had found its mark. He slid from his horse and walked cautiously into the bramble.

From behind a tree, a bear of a man crashed toward him so swiftly that Geoffrey had no time to react. They sprawled upon the thick carpet of vines. The crushing weight of the larger man squeezed the air from Geoffrey's lungs.

The man reached for Geoffrey's throat with his left hand. His strength would have been overwhelming had he not been hampered by the bullet Geoffrey had sent into his right arm.

Geoffrey struggled to breathe. His hand grasped wildly among the vines. Finding a rock, he brought it down with all the force he could manage upon his assailant's head.

The man fell limp. Geoffrey rolled out from beneath him, panting. He caught his breath and surveyed the still form of the ruddy-faced hulk.

The blow that would have killed most men had only rendered this man unconscious. Except for the wound that seeped red on his forearm, he might have been in a deep sleep. Geoffrey had seen similar injuries during battle. Should the man awaken in the next few hours, the loss of blood and a painful wound would occupy his attention.

He hurried back to the path. He could not yet count himself the victor. He had Caroline yet to find and rescue.

When yet another morning broke with her in captivity, Caroline thought she would go mad with worry and fatigue. She slept little at night. The sound of rats scurrying about the filthy room kept her awake.

Lord Humphrey had told her about the note. Geoffrey would come soon, he assured her each morning when he brought her a meager breakfast. And after Geoffrey was out of the way, she would belong to him.

She shivered in the chill of early morning. The fire had gone low during the night. She struggled to stir up the embers.

Lord Humphrey entered. He closed the door tightly behind him. "Cold, my pet? I cannot have my future bride taking a chill. Let me help you with the fire."

As he bent to stoke the wood, Caroline edged toward the table. Grasping a large mug in her bound hands, she edged toward the Viscount. If she could render him unconscious, she could escape, and perhaps warn Geoffrey.

At the upward movement of her arms, the Viscount spun. He avoided the blow, which sent Caroline, now off balance, plummeting into the hard stone wall of the fireplace.

He grasped her roughly by the shoulders and shook her. "You would do me harm? You had better change your ways or I shall see that you come to the same end as your love."

He flung her onto the floor, where she collapsed in a

weary heap. Feeling weak and helpless, she gave into her anguish and wept, uncontrollable sobs shaking her shoulders.

He stared down at her. "You look a bit pale. Perhaps you have not gotten enough rest. Do not waste your time pining for your love. It will do neither of you any good."

He nudged her with the toe of his boot. "I have the fire stoked to a blaze. I shall come back later with your lunch. And I shall bring a trophy, a glove perhaps, from your former suitor."

He closed the door and latched it behind him.

So deep was Caroline's despair that she heard nothing except the sound of her own sobs. She continued for some time, not bothering to pick herself up from the mud floor. Nothing seemed to matter now. If the Viscount succeeded in his plans, she no longer cared what became of her.

The crackling above her head inspired only a vague curiosity. Yet, as it grew louder, she glanced up. Flames licked at the thatched roof. Sparks from the grimy chimney had caught the roof on fire. Smoke filled the room.

Seized by panic, Caroline pounded at the door. "Open the door! Oh please, let me out!"

She climbed to the window and pried at the bars. She had little hope of budging them, yet less hope of escaping out the heavy, bolted door.

Orange tongues of flame danced along the beam above her head. The smoke thickened. Caroline began to cough.

Suddenly, she heard someone call out her name. She turned toward the sound, gasping for breath. Sparks danced through the air, lighting upon the wood table and setting it ablaze.

The acrid smell of smoke filled her nostrils. Remaining conscious became a struggle.

A hand seized her and cast her toward the door. She recognized Lord Humphrey's voice urging her to hurry.

She stumbled and he grasped her under the arms, shoving her toward the doorway. She saw the welcome light of outdoors and stumbled toward it, sucking in deep mouthfuls of air.

The sound of hoofbeats pounded and Geoffrey sprang from his horse. He knelt beside her. "Caroline, are you alright?"

His voice sounded as though he were far away.

"Lord Humphrey is still inside."

Geoffrey hesitated for a moment. A mix of emotions played across his face. Then he turned and bolted toward the burning structure.

Caroline moaned softly, rocking herself upon the ground. "No, Geoffrey . . ."

He emerged, dragging the unconscious figure of the Viscount. Moments later, the roof collapsed in a roar of flames.

Geoffrey abandoned the Viscount and took Caroline in his arms. "Are you hurt?"

Caroline buried her head against his smoky coat and sobbed. "I thought I would never see you again. He meant to kill you. He told me he would bring your glove as proof you were dead."

"Hush, hush." He cradled her gently. "I am here, alive and well. But we must get you away from here."

Caroline glanced at the still figure lying on the ground. A gash on Lord Humphrey's forehead trailed across his face.

"Is he dead?"

Geoffrey pulled her to her feet.

"No. I will send Nottington back for him."

He led her toward Victory and helped her mount. He swung up behind her and urged the horse back along the path. Caroline thought it ironic that she had always wanted to ride this horse, and now she was too weary to care.

For two days she drifted in and out of sleep, aware only that voices and faces seemed to appear and then fade out of focus. At last, she opened her eyes to see Lavenia sitting at her side.

"Thank goodness, Caroline. I thought you would simply never wake. You must try to eat. You are nearly skin and bones."

Caroline smiled weakly. "I am glad to be back."

The memories came back to her. "Geoffrey? Is he alright?"

"He is fine."

"And the Viscount?"

"I am afraid he was not so fortunate. His eyes were badly burned by the cinders. The burns on his face will heal, but I am afraid he will be blind."

Caroline shuddered.

"You must not worry about him. Mother and I have worried only about you since we returned from London yesterday and heard what you had been through. It must have been terrible for you."

"It *was* terrible. I thought that Geoffrey would surely die."

Lavenia nodded. "He told us his true identity. I can see why he wished to hide the truth from Lord Humphrey."

She patted Caroline's arm. "I am going to order you some lunch. You must rest quietly until it arrives."

Caroline glanced about the quiet room, relieved to be back in the home she loved. If only she could see Geoffrey, she would feel completely at peace.

Lady Aberly joined her while she ate lunch and drank a reviving cup of tea.

"I feel so much better. I think I shall dress and sit out in the garden," Caroline said.

"The fresh air and sun would do you good, if you are up to going out. You are very pale from remaining indoors during your imprisonment. And I know a young man who has been asking to see you as soon as you are able to abide company."

Caroline ran her hand across her tousled hair. "Would you see if Maggie might come do something about my appearance?"

Lady Aberly smiled warmly. "I shall do so gladly."

When Maggie's ministrations were performed to her satisfaction, Caroline strolled down to the garden. She was not surprised, but quite thrilled to see Geoffrey waiting.

He took her in his arms. "I feared for your life."

She looked up into his eyes. "And I yours. Lord Humphrey planned to use me as the bait to lure you to your death. I wanted to warn you. It nearly drove me mad that I had no way out of the cottage."

He ran a gentle hand across her hair. "It is all over now. The Viscount will be leaving soon. I shall explain the particulars tomorrow."

"He is here then?"

Geoffrey nodded. "I had him brought here to recover from his burns."

"I understand that he was blinded after he rescued me. It was probably the most noble thing he has ever done."

"For that rescue he shall be rewarded with his freedom. Had any harm come to you, I would see him face his full punishment."

They sat together in the garden while Lady Aberly sat at the open parlor door, where she had a clear view as chaperon.

Caroline remembered what Lavenia had said. "They know all about you. Lavenia told me you admitted to them that you are the heir. Do they know about me?"

"No. And they shall not, although except for their position in society, there is little difference between you. You see, Lady Aberly was a friend of Lady Eleanor, not a relative. Lady Aberly's husband was given to his liquor and games of chance, not unlike Lord Humphrey. When he died, it was discovered that the estate was heavily in debt."

Caroline sucked in her breath. "Lady Aberly and Lavenia had nothing?"

"Exactly. To spare her good friend the embarrassment, Lady Eleanor brought her here and allowed her to pretend she was related. It seemed she was wont to help those she loved, no matter what their circumstance."

Tears filled Caroline's eyes. "She was a very great lady."

He captured a hand and kissed the tip of each finger. "I shall always be grateful to her for her kind heart that allowed me to meet you. And I am glad that I can court you openly, Caroline. It makes things much less awkward."

"Indeed. Though I see Lady Aberly is keeping a close watch."

He laughed. "Lady Aberly was quite embarrassed to learn of my real position. She made things right by immediately inviting me to join the family for supper tonight."

"And Lord Humphrey?"

"He shall stay in his quarters?"

"And then?"

Geoffrey would say no more regarding the Viscount. He insisted she wait until Lord Humphrey should join them in the morning.

Caroline spent a happy evening in Geoffrey's company despite her curiosity about the fate of Lord Humphrey.

The next morning, Edwards led the Viscount carefully down the stairs to join them in the drawing room. Caroline shuddered. His bandaged eyes reminded her of the fire that had caused his injury.

When they had all settled, Geoffrey began to speak.

"It must be decided, Lord Humphrey, what shall be done with you. By all rights, I should call in the constable and have you imprisoned for the rest of your life. But I am loath to do so considering the injury that you have suffered. The fact that you will live from now on, with the consequence of your misdeed, stands for something."

The Viscount gave a bitter laugh. "How ironic you should save *my* life only to leave me blinded."

"Your own choices led to your misfortune. I take no credit for that. What I shall do is allow you to return to the Royal Crescent and pack your things. You shall go abroad and not return. I think, due to the condition you are in, Lady Eleanor would have had no objection to allowing me to furnish you a small pension from my inheritance, only enough to live on. If you ever return, you shall lose your freedom. Do you agree?"

"It seems I have no choice."

Geoffrey motioned to Edwards. "Take him away. Have Nottington drive him to Bath and make sure he takes passage as I have arranged."

"Yes, my lord."

When the Viscount had been led away, Lady Aberly declared, "I am glad this business is all settled so that we may get peacefully on with the business of a wedding."

Geoffrey offered Caroline his arm. "Two weddings, I believe." He winked at her. "Do you agree, my lady?"

She smiled. "As you wish, my lord." She took his arm and silently blessed Lady Eleanor for giving a chambermaid a chance to become a lady.